They had him boxed in

Cade saw a narrow alley coming up. It was only wide enough to take one car at a time. He jammed his foot down hard on the gas pedal, feeling the powerful supercharged cruiser leap forward.

Behind him, the rattle of gunfire rose above the screaming engine, and the rear window imploded as a stream of slugs shattered the glass. As the car careered into the alley, he caught a glimpse of the limousine following him. Then he felt the cruiser lurch as a rear tire blew. Moments later, the other one went, and the vehicle screeched along on steel rims.

Cade snatched up the SPAS, released the door latch and slammed on the brake. He exited the slithering car, braced his back against the wall and swung the SPAS into position. He triggered the autoloader without pause, and the limousine's windshield disintegrated under the barrage.

CADE

MIKE LINAKER

Darksiders

A GOLD EAGLE BOOK FROM
WORLDWIDE®

TORONTO • NEW YORK • LONDON
AMSTERDAM • PARIS • SYDNEY • HAMBURG
STOCKHOLM • ATHENS • TOKYO • MILAN
MADRID • WARSAW • BUDAPEST • AUCKLAND

First edition May 1992

ISBN 0-373-63804-3

DARKSIDERS

Copyright © 1992 by Mike Linaker.
Philippine copyright 1992. Australian copyright 1992.

Printed in U.S.A.

Darksiders

1

The instant the soft tone of the com unit in his pocket told Cade that his partner was in position at the rear of the warehouse, he moved in, leading with the big .357 Magnum autopistol in his right hand.

He hit the side door with his shoulder, feeling the rusting steel panel cave in. The door slammed against the inside wall with a hollow crash, dislodging years of accumulated dust and flakes of concrete.

The interior was lit by a few stark tube lights suspended from the overhead beams. They gave enough illumination for Cade to pinpoint the dealers and buyers who were bunched around the open trunk of a Buick Rocket he had followed in from Syracuse.

The moment Cade barreled through the door, all interest in the deal was lost.

"Freeze!" Cade shouted. "Justice Department! Nobody move!"

The man who had sat behind the Buick's wheel yelled something unintelligible and swiveled in Cade's direction. He dragged a sawed-off Remington Auto 12-gauge from under his leather coat and opened up without warning.

Cade took a long dive, hitting the concrete floor on his left shoulder. He rolled frantically, hearing the Remington blast out shot after shot. Powdery concrete dusted the air as the slugs left a pockmarked trail on the warehouse floor.

Coming to a halt against an overturned fuel drum, Cade gathered his legs under him and powered up off the floor in a single motion. The autopistol rose with him, tracking in on the shotgunner. Cade pulled back on the trigger, feeling the power of the heavy weapon as it fired. The hollowpoint caught the dealer in the left chest, high up. The expanding slug took away a chunk of flesh as it ripped through his body, and his left arm lost all its strength. It sagged uselessly at his side. The dealer let out a yell of pain and rage, and despite his pain, he tried to take out Cade with the Remington held one-handed. But the .357 beat him to it, the second slug catching him between the eyes and snapping his head back in a mist of dark blood.

As the dealer tumbled to the floor, Cade swept the Magnum across his body, triggering at a swarthy-looking man with a subgun who emerged from the cover of the Buick's trunk. The subgun began to crackle, but Cade's bullets had already found their mark, and the subgun expended its load into the floor. The weapon's owner flopped back against the car, his chest glistening with spreading blood.

The rest of the group had split apart and were seeking escape routes, covering themselves with occasional bursts. Two of them headed for the far end of the warehouse, and Cade ignored these. His partner would deal with them.

He concentrated on the remaining two. They clearly weren't in the right frame of mind to give themselves up. They had been busted in the act of dealing in illegal weapons. That meant a nonnegotiable term of hard time on the Mars Project, helping construct the first city and space port on one of the off-world shuttle platforms. Nobody with any sense left inside their skull was going to chance that. It was worth the risk trying to escape. Even a slug from the gun of a Justice marshal was preferable.

Cade took off after the pair, aware that they both were armed.

They crashed their way through pyramids of crates, then Cade saw them veer to one side, heading for the deeper shadows along the wall. He followed, dodging in and out among boxes and crates, quick and light on his feet.

Gunfire winked out of the shadows, and Cade altered his line of travel. Bullets whined against the steelwork of the warehouse supports, sparks flashing briefly. Cade returned fire, his target pinpointed by the muzzle-flash.

"Over here!" one of the suspects yelled.

The shout was followed by an echoing crash. An oblong of pale light broke the darkness.

Cade quickly realized that they had found a door and were going to make a break for it. Their chances had just improved by fifty percent, he thought grimly.

He followed, ignoring the risk. As he reached the open door, an autoweapon crackled from the outer darkness. Cade ducked low, feeling the door frame shudder as a hail of high-powered slugs struck it.

He dived through the door, breaking right, almost on his knees. He peered into the gloom of the deserted alley, breathing in the stench of decay. Up ahead he caught the rattle of scurrying feet. Turning in that direction, he spotted his suspects. He powered after them, his finger ready on the trigger, ready to draw a bead when he had a second's chance.

They were heading for the distant mouth of the alley, where bright neon lights created a rainbow of color out of the darkness. There was noise, too, and movement. Cade swore angrily as he realized where the suspects were heading.

The alley opened up onto Chinatown. If they mingled with the teeming crowds, he would lose them. And he had no intention of doing that. He had spent almost two whole weeks building up to the night's confrontation, living and breathing in New York's lower levels. Cade did not like losing out on a bust. He took it personally.

He never knew why one of the running men stopped to fire at him. If he had kept going the way his partner did, he might have escaped. But when he was only a few yards from the mouth of the alley, the man suddenly swiveled around. The dark SMG in his hands rose, spitting flame as he triggered it at the pursuing officer.

Cade felt slugs chew at the collar of his jacket as he twisted to one side. He banged up against the wall, then regained his balance and threw up the autopistol. His finger worked the trigger in rapid fire, the .357's muzzle flicking up. Shell casings rang sharply against the floor of the alley.

The suspect threw his arms wide, backpedaling out of control. His chest and throat pumped blood. He gave a scared cry and fell back, his body shuddering uncontrollably as the shock effect of the slugs ravaged his nervous system.

Cade fed a fresh clip into the pistol and jacked the slide back to cock it, then ran past the dying man.

Ahead of him the Chinatown crowd scattered, alarmed by the rattle of gunfire.

Cade burst from the alley into the noise and color of the street. Cars were lined up fender to fender as they inched through the busy thoroughfare.

Chinatown, New York, 2052, hadn't changed much in the past hundred years. The inhabitants still respected many of the old ways and chose to follow the more deeply rooted traditions and customs that had served China for a thousand years. But they were children of technology, too, and side by side with the old ways, relied on some of the most advanced machines and processes of the time. Among the hand-painted signs and delicate filigrees of Chinese decorations were neon lights and holographic advertisements. The electronic wizardry of the twenty-first century was artfully blended with the subtle finery of the Chinese artisans. Street stalls still sold herbal medicines, and the fortune-teller's bird picked out the customer's future from a pile of cards. In the shop corners and smoky rooms the old men played endless games of mah-jongg, clicking and shuffling the ivory blocks to sudden cries of excitement or sharp rebukes. Outside, the misty air, hazed by a myriad collection of lights, brought the sounds and scents of China to New York's crowded streets. Steam from pots of boiling noodles mingled with the aromas of black-bean sauce, bowls of rich lobster and chicken stew. Above the noise rose the ever-present, shrill cadences of traditional Chinese popular songs, the strident tones delivering the age-old message of the community. It was now, as it had always been, a determination to contain the values of the past within the strictures of the present.

Cade spotted his quarry as in his haste the man collided with a battered delivery van, his handgun bouncing from his hand. He went down on his knees, searching for the weapon, but a passerby's foot caught the autopistol and sent it skittering across the street. It slid under a parked car. Realizing he was wasting time, the man hauled himself to his feet, throwing a panicked glance at the tall lawman bearing down on him. He turned to run just as Cade reached him.

A big hand grabbed hold of his coat, pulling him back and bouncing him off the side of a passing car. The driver leaned out to protest, then decided against it when he saw the .357 in Cade's hand.

The suspect was wild-eyed and charged up with adrenaline. He snatched for the switchblade he carried under his coat. He thumbed the button and the blade clicked into place.

"Have a taste of this!" he yelled at Cade, lunging forward with the knife.

Cade hardly appeared to have moved. His left fist, bunched into a hard ball, arced round in a vicious half circle. It connected with the suspect's jaw. Blood spurted from torn lips. The suspect went down hard, bouncing as he hit the street.

Cade picked up the switchblade and closed it. He dropped the weapon into his pocket before he bent over the dazed man and yanked him to his feet, then propped him against the side of the delivery van. The man stared at him through glazed eyes. His mouth was slack, dribbling blood.

At the sight of blood, whispers and complaints started up from the crowd that had started to close around them.

Cade pulled out his leather badge-holder and held it up where everyone could see it.

"Justice marshal," he announced. "This is an arrest. Everyone, keep moving on."

The jostling crowd quieted and began to break up. The Justice marshals, as they had been quickly tagged after their inception, had a tough reputation, and they backed it with hard action against anyone who interfered with their business.

Cade holstered his gun and pulled a pair of plasti-cuffs from his pocket. He snapped them on the suspect's wrists.

"You could have made this easy on both of us," Cade said. "I got better things to do than chasing dopeheads like you all over New York."

The man merely stared at him, his face expressionless.

"You going to tell me you want your rights read?" Cade asked. "No chance. This cop doesn't play by NYPD rules.

Couple of days, and you'll be on your way to the Mars Project for a stretch.''

Awareness fired the man's eyes. He swallowed hard, then coughed as he tasted blood in his throat.

"Maybe we can deal," he said, his eyes searching Cade's for a reaction.

"No deals."

"Yeah? But I can give you an earful...real interesting stuff. Come on, man, I don't need a vacation in space. You could recommend me for one of the farms. Huh? Am I right?''

The shrill sound of a NYPD patrol cruiser told Cade the local police were on their way. He could see the flashing roof light moving slowly along the street.

"Well?" Cade prompted.

"Make a deal first," the suspect pleaded.

"Don't stretch your luck, pal," Cade warned. He pulled a battered pack of thin cigars from his inside pocket. Lighting up, he glanced at the suspect. The man was sweating heavily, breathing noisily through his nose. He spit blood from his battered mouth.

"I got information about the missing Darksiders," he said.

Cade frowned. "What missing Darksiders? Don't feed me some made-up fool's story. I don't have much patience this late in the day."

"Check with the local PD. The Darksiders have been vanishing for the last six months. Not just one or two—I'm talking big numbers."

"Where do you tie in?"

"I don't," the suspect said. "It's just 'cause I know the Darksiders. Used to spend some time with them when I was on the skids. I heard talk, and saw a couple of things. It's no scam.''

The sleek shape of the armored patrol cruiser rolled to a stop alongside Cade. The uniformed policemen climbed out. They were big, hard-eyed individuals, wearing regulation body armor.

"Who the hell are you?'' demanded the lead man. His name tag identified him as Treat.

Not liking his attitude, Cade ignored him.

"Hey, I asked a question.''

Cade sensed Treat's partner moving in behind him. "Tell your partner to step out where I can see him,'' Cade said, allowing a hard edge to sharpen his words.

Treat smiled. His right hand dropped to the thick butt of the handgun holstered on his hip. He stared directly at Cade.

"Doesn't appear to me you're in any position to make demands,'' he said.

"Don't make book on that,'' Cade said lazily, and showed Treat his badge. He enjoyed the dumb expression that filtered across Treat's broad face. "Now tell your partner to make front and center before I do something we'll all regret in the morning.''

Treat jerked his head. His partner walked around to join him. Cade repeated his badge trick. Treat's partner was bigger and broader. He had a bristling mustache over his upper lip. He took a long look at Cade's badge, shaking his head slowly.

"I think you marshals are a crock of shit,'' he said.

"Thinking like that could be harmful to your health, Dolan,'' Cade said, checking the cop's name tag.

"Yeah?''

"Yeah,'' Cade answered, then shrugged and changed the subject.

"You know him?" Cade asked, indicating his prisoner.

Treat nodded. "Bernie Stenner. Part of the local night-life, and a dedicated dopehead. Into every dirty deal going. All small-time stuff."

"Well, Bernie has graduated to bigger things," Cade said. "I just busted Bernie and his friends doing a deal with stolen autoweapons."

He indicated the alley across the street.

"One of Bernie's partners is in there. You'll find more in the old warehouse at the far end. There's a Buick Rocket inside with a trunk full of guns that came in from Canada. I want you to call in and get a crew down here. Close off the warehouse and have your people go over the car. See what else they can pick up from it."

"What about him?" Treat asked, jerking a thumb at Bernie.

"Just book him at the station," Cade said. "I want to talk to him later. We're developing a real relationship, right, Bernie?"

Stenner nodded unhappily, staring down at the ground between his feet.

"You need me, I'll be in the warehouse," Cade said. "I want to check out my partner."

He made his way across the street and along the alley. He didn't even bother to look at the motionless figure of the man he'd dropped in the alley. Cade knew he was dead.

He stepped back inside the warehouse and hurried across to the abandoned car. The trunk was still open. A tall figure was bending over it, examining the contents.

"You get those two I sent you?" Cade asked.

His partner straightened up as Cade neared the car. His eyes were fixed on the cigar Cade was smoking. He didn't say anything, but then, he didn't have to. The message, the annoying message, was all too clear.

Irritation soured the taste of the cigar. Cade snatched it from his lips and tossed it to the ground.

"You do that every time," he said. "I just start enjoying one of the damn things, and you do it every time."

"Do what, T.J.?"

"Don't play innocent with me, Janek," Cade said. "You give me that goddamn look. That full-of-pity expression."

"Please yourself," Janek snapped. "Burn out your lungs if you want." He pointed to the rear of the warehouse.

"The two suspects who eluded you are down there. One's dead. The other merely unconscious. I cuffed him."

"Read them their rights?" Cade asked with undisguised sarcasm.

"That would have proved a futile exercise," Janek said stiffly. "The dead one's past caring. The other one was unconscious at the time."

Cade repressed a grin, then turned away slightly to conceal his amusement.

But Janek hadn't been fooled. "Did I say something to amuse you, Thomas?" he asked. He only used Cade's full name when he was annoyed.

Cade didn't reply. Instead he moved to the Buick's trunk and gazed down at the stacked Uzi Model-400s. The powerful autoweapons, capable of terrible rates of fire and fitted with laser sights, were banned from private ownership. They were prized weapons, much sought after by the criminal fraternity, and like anything banned, they had gained notoriety. Headquarters had picked up information of a shipment coming in from Canada. Cade and his partner had been assigned to the case. They had followed the shipment in from Canada down to New York, to the point of delivery.

"Enough weaponry there to start a small war," Cade said quietly. "If we left these street gangs to themselves, they'd wipe themselves out. The problem is they'd take half New York with them."

The ploy of changing the subject didn't seem to work, as Janek pursued his line of questioning. "Thomas, did I say something to amuse you?" asked Janek.

Cade turned to stare at the tall figure. He was six feet tall himself, but Janek topped him by two inches. Short-cropped white-blond hair crowned the towering, perfect body, above an impassive face. Janek was in his serious mood.

Cade sighed. This was something he was going to have to work on. Janek's sense of humor was conspicuous by its absence. Usually it didn't bother Cade all that much. He'd got used to Janek's dry approach. But there were times when a little lighthearted banter would have been welcome.

On the face of it, there were a whole lot of reasons for having a dedicated cyborg for a partner. Cade and Janek worked well together. The only objection Cade did have was with the lack of foresight shown by the technicians at Cybo Tech when they had failed to include a fully developed sense of humor in Janek's function modes.

Janek was capable of impressive feats—physical and mental—but during their two years together Cade had never heard his robot partner laugh out loud.

2

It was after midnight when Cade wheeled the travel-stained Ford Turbo-6 into the parking lot behind the police precinct house in the shadow of Manhattan Bridge. He cut the engine and climbed out. He stood beside the car, stretching tiredly. It had been a long day. The drive from Syracuse, trailing the Buick with its load of guns, had been frustratingly slow. The subsequent running battle with the suspects hadn't been the kind of ending to the day that Cade would have chosen.

But that was the way life ran. It was frequently a bitch. And he couldn't complain. He had been told from the start that a Justice marshal commission was no ticket to an easy ride. That had been just about the only true thing he had been told.

The opposite door banged shut, and Janek came around to join him, looking as fresh as ever. Time of day or night meant nothing to the cyborg. He never looked worn-out. Which sometimes hurt like hell.

"Let's go and get this over with," Cade said, unable to hold back the edginess from his voice.

"Is something bothering you?" Janek asked, concern showing in his modulated tone.

Cade grimaced. *Here we go. Now it's mother-hen time.*

"Yeah, Janek," he replied as they walked up the steps into the precinct house. "I'm tired. Hungry. I want to hit the sack, but instead I have to talk to this guy, Stenner, because he says he has some information."

"I could do that for you, T.J. You could go to the apartment and I could let you know in the morning what I found out."

"Yeah? Now, why didn't I think of that?" But Cade didn't pause.

He strode on inside the station and up to the night desk.

There were a few uniformed officers hanging around as shifts changed. In among the human officers were a number of KC-200 androids. The robot patrolmen stood waiting patiently for their assignments.

The grizzled desk sergeant on duty eyed the Justice marshal with a less than favorable stare. "What?" he barked.

Before Cade could reply, Janek made a disapproving sound, shaking his head. "Is that the way you deal with the public? It isn't hard to realize why the police have such a lack of cooperation from..."

The sergeant half rose from his seat. His beefy face had turned a darker shade of red. "Hey, Jack, you want I should come round there and lay one on you?"

Cade took out his badge and stuck it under the enraged sergeant's nose.

"My partner's had a long day," he said. "On the other hand, I can't exactly blame him."

The Justice Department shield had already taken effect. Still angry, but subdued, the sergeant sat down. He glared around the room, daring anyone to make a comment, then returned his attention to Cade.

"Okay, Marshal, what can I do for you?"

"You got a couple of cruiser cops who brought in a prisoner earlier. Treat and Dolan."

"You the one who busted those gunrunners? Yeah, they took him upstairs to the holding tank. Second floor."

Cade headed for the elevator, with Janek following silently behind him.

"That sergeant should be reported," Janek stated flatly.

"And you should be melted down and processed into cans," Cade snapped. "How many times do I have to tell you? Don't do that."

"Thomas..."

"And don't use that tone with me. I know your game, Janek. Make *me* feel guilty when it's you who shot off his mouth."

Janek's impassive features formed into a puzzled frown. "What does 'shot off his mouth' mean, T.J.? It's not a logical expression."

"As far as logic goes, pal, you are way off base," Cade said. "Do me a favor tonight, Janek. Flip to your mean-cop mode and make life easy for me. Okay?"

Janek merely shrugged. He had never quite managed to master the movement fully, and it always came out lopsided.

The elevator lurched to a stop, and the doors opened in fits and starts. They emerged in a featureless corridor that stank of disinfectant and a whole range of body smells. The concrete floor echoed as they made their way to the electronic door at the far end. Cade punched the key that activated the vid-screen.

"What's your business?" asked the guard as his face appeared on the tube.

"T. J. Cade. Justice marshal." Cade held his badge to the ID grid. The grid scanned his badge, picking up the bar code.

"And the other one," the guard said.

Janek in turn placed his badge to the grid.

"A cybo?" The guard's bored expression lightened. "Hey, maybe the scanner is a relative of yours." He chuckled at his own joke and looked at Cade, obviously expecting a response.

"Just open the damn door," Cade snapped. "And be careful what you say about my partner. He hasn't had his plugs changed for a week and he's getting touchy."

The door slid open, allowing them through.

"What plugs, T.J.?" Janek asked, but Cade ignored him.

They reached the desk. The guard smirked at Janek, but didn't say anything.

"You've got a suspect in the tank. Name of Stenner. Couple of beat cops brought him in earlier. I collared him on a gunrunning charge. I need to talk to him."

The guard's expression changed. He suddenly looked uncomfortable.

"Is there a problem?" Janek asked sharply, picking up on the guard's unease.

The guy glanced at Janek, not liking the hard gleam in his gray eyes. He turned to Cade, expecting a little comfort from a fellow human. He was wrong. Cade's expression was colder than his partner's.

"Lost your voice, pal? I'd get it back fast unless you want trouble."

"Well, ah, he's no longer here," the guard replied. "These suits from the Urban Crime Squad came and took Stenner away about an hour ago. They had the paperwork. Nothing I could do."

"Where did they take him?" Cade asked.

"I didn't ask. They didn't say. You don't fuck with the UCS."

Cade leaned across the desk. "You got that wrong. What you don't fuck with is a Justice marshal."

He turned and strode away, with his partner on his heels. Janek didn't speak until they were back in the elevator. "What does the Urban Crime Squad want with Stenner?" he asked.

"Good question."

"I know, T.J. That's why I asked it. Now answer me."

"How the hell do I know?" Cade said, but he was beginning to smell something bad going down. "Get me the number for UCS."

Somewhere in Janek's brain, memory chips searched for the required number. "Area code..." Janek began.

"Just the damn number, not the history of the New York telephone system," Cade growled. He was not in the mood for one of Janek's intricate replies to a simple question.

"There are times, Thomas, when I fail to understand your surliness. You should learn to control your inner feelings when dealing with people."

"You know your problem? You just don't know when to shut up."

"I find it's better to bring these things into the open. Why bottle them up? Talk to me, T.J. Describe your feelings at this present time."

Cade grinned suddenly. "Don't tempt me, Janek. Just don't ask."

"Can we talk about it later?"

"Much later," Cade muttered to himself, forgetting Janek's highly sensitive hearing.

"Fine, T.J. Later."

The desk sergeant eyed them warily as they emerged from the elevator.

"Why didn't you tell me the UCS had dealt themselves into this business?" Cade asked.

The sergeant held his ground. "One, you didn't ask. Two, I don't interfere with the UCS."

"Did you know they took Stenner away?"

"Hey, they didn't come through here with him."

"He knows, T.J.," Janek said.

"That's twice you got up my nose tonight," the sergeant said. "You are pissing me off."

"I'm all shook up about that," Janek said.

"What's with him?" the sergeant asked.

"He means you don't scare him," Cade explained, realizing that the sergeant wasn't aware he was dealing with a cyborg. "Did you know the UCS men?"

"What? No. Never seen 'em before. All I got was their names. Pair called Feldstet and Miles. Couple of charmers."

"Where do they hang out?"

"UCS building up near Brooklyn Park."

"I need a phone," Cade said.

The sergeant jerked a thumb in the direction of a closed door. "Empty office there."

Janek followed Cade and closed the office door behind them. Cade sat down behind the cluttered desk and picked up the receiver. The vid-screen on the unit flickered to life. As he punched in the UCS number, Janek reached out and put the first finger of his left hand on the unit's input cable. Delicate sensors just below his artificial skin picked up the electronic signals pulsing through the cables and transmitted them to his electronic receiving banks.

A woman's face appeared on the vid-screen.

"UCS. How can I help you?"

The uniformity in her voice told Cade she was a cyborg.

"Justice Marshal Cade. I need to speak to whoever is in charge."

"Just a moment, Marshal Cade."

Cade glanced at Janek. "You'd like her," he said. "She's just your type, Janek."

The cyborg's face expressed contempt for the remark. "This base reduction of everything to sexual innuendo is so immature, Thomas," he said in his most patronizing tone.

"Yeah, I know," Cade said. "Great, isn't it?"

The vid-screen filed with static, cleared, and Cade found himself looking at a broad-faced man with hard, unflinching eyes.

"Captain Connor," he identified himself. "What can I do for you, Cade?"

"Two of your people stopped by the Manhattan Bridge precinct house a while ago and took away a suspect being held for me. I'd like to know why. And just who the hell overrode my authority?"

"Who were the officers?"

"Feldstet and Miles," Cade told him.

"I can tell you they operate out of here," Connor affirmed, "but I can't help you more than that. I haven't heard a thing about any prisoner being pulled in by our people. You sure about this, Marshal?"

"Do I look like I just came off the farm?"

"I wasn't suggesting..."

"If I were you, Connor, I'd run a check on Feldstet and Miles. Maybe they're doing a little moonlighting. Could be your squad needs a visit from the Justice Department. Tighten up, Connor, or I'll have it done for you."

Cade broke the connection, slamming down the receiver. He slumped back in the swivel seat, pulling his pack of cigars from his pocket. He lit one, his glance defying Janek to say a word.

"So?" he asked.

"Connor was recording the conversation, T.J.," Janek said.

Cade smiled. "This had really looked like nothing as much as a waste of my time with Stenner. But it is getting to look as though it will be worth my while. So maybe, after all, he hadn't just made a wild shot in the dark about the Darksiders. Someone got wind of Stenner wanting to talk, and they don't seem anxious to have that happen."

"Whoever these people are, they clearly have police officers on their payroll."

"We live in a wicked world."

"Do you think Connor's in with Feldstet and Miles? Or was he just covering his back by recording your conversation?"

"I figure we'll find out soon enough." Cade leaned forward and picked up the phone again.

"Who are you calling now?"

"This one's personal," Cade said. "You go and find a computer terminal and plug yourself in. I want everything you can find on Feldstet and Miles, and also anything about missing Darksiders."

Janek nodded. He turned and left the office.

Cade watched the vid-screen. It remained blank as the call was connected. The moment it was through, the screen was filled with a text message:

"This number is temporarily disconnected."

"Damn!" Cade muttered. He broke the connection and punched in a new number. The vid-screen showed a tired, unshaven face. "This is Tom Cade, I want to speak to Kate Bannion."

"She's not here."

"Not in the office or not in the building?" Cade asked.

"She's on a special assignment for the paper. Can't be contacted."

The connection was cut, and Cade was left staring at the blank screen.

"Smithereens," he grumbled.

What was Kate up to now?

It would be something crazy, he knew.

In all the time he had known Kate Bannion, she had never been content to work on anything ordinary. Every story she went after for the *New York Century* was either controversial or dangerous. She enjoyed a challenge. Thrived on risk. It was the reason he liked her. Liked? What the hell, he thought, it was the reason he wanted her. He'd never known any woman quite like her. Or loved any woman like her.

"Thomas!"

Cade glanced up and saw Janek standing in the doorway.

"Yeah?"

"I have the information."

"Good. Let's go. You can give me a rundown in the car."

"Where are we going?" Janek asked on their way to the front doors.

Cade pushed through the station doors and went down the steps. "You got addresses for Feldstet and Miles?"

"Of course," Janek replied stiffly. "You asked me to get them, so I did. You shouldn't need to question my reliability, Thomas. I'm not a domestic cybo. I can think for myself."

"Yeah? Well, think while you drive," Cade said. He tossed the car keys to Janek. "Time you started earning your keep. Those fancy clothes you wear don't grow on damn trees."

"Naturally," Janek said with his robotic logic. "Only wood grows on trees."

"Just drive, smart-ass."

Janek rolled the car out onto the street.

"Miles is the closest," he said.

"Let's go, hotshot."

Janek, as always, drove perfectly but fast. His advanced intelligence and control allowed him to anticipate far ahead of any human driver. He could judge road and vehicle conditions to a precise point. It meant that he could drive to the limit and still be in control. When he had first partnered Cade, the cyborg's driving had scared the hell out of his human companion. After two years Cade was well used to Janek's driving and trusted him to a degree he never would have trusted a human partner.

They cut across to Roosevelt Drive, flanking the murky strip of the East River. Mist blanketed the dirty water. In the distance foghorns threw their mournful cries out of the gloom. Whatever changes transformed the city, the river remained constant.

The muggy night sky over the city glowed with multicolored light. Gigantic advertising vid-screens, fixed to the sides of buildings, threw out their eternal consumer messages, everything from the latest-model cars to forthcoming attractions on one of New York's hologram-TV channels.

Janek gave Cade a word-by-word rundown on Feldstet and Miles. The official biographies gave no indication of any suspicious dealings involving the two officers, but Cade wouldn't have expected anything else. Police officers who had gone dirty were usually clever enough to keep their clandestine activities off the record. Feldstet and Miles warranted some closer examination.

Before Janek started on the Darksider information, he took a look in the rearview mirror and made a soft sound that was a confirmation of something he'd been checking.

"We have tails," he informed Cade. "Closing fast. A dark blue Chevrolet and a gray Buick. I've been monitoring them, just to be sure."

"And?"

"I'm sure, T.J."

Cade sighed. He reached for the combat shotgun clipped between the front seats. The Franchi-SPAS Model 16 had remained the most formidable combat weapon of its type for over sixty years. Its basic design, originated in Italy, had never been bettered. Now it was standard issue for law agencies, and in the right hands its destructive power was formidable. Cade checked that the weapon was fully loaded, making sure that the laser sight was functioning. He counted the extra shells in the ammo rack under the dash.

"Your side, T.J.," Janek warned. He jammed his foot hard on the gas, sending them hurtling forward. Tires screeched in protest as the pursuing car swept around the Ford's rear, its front bumper scraping the fender. Janek gripped the wheel, keeping the swaying car on line.

Cade rolled down his window as the Buick roared alongside. He caught a glimpse of hunched figures inside the darkened vehicle. Light glanced off the barrels of weapons as they were thrust into view. Then autoweapons opened up, and streams of slugs hammered the Ford's bodywork. A rear window imploded, filling the interior with glass particles.

Gritting his teeth against the buffeting wind, Cade aimed the SPAS. He triggered two shots, blasting the 12-gauge steel shot into the Buick's front tire. The rubber blew with a harsh sound, dropping the car onto its steel rim. A long tail of bright sparks flew up from the rim. The Buick slipped away, careering back and forth across the lanes as the driver fought the heavy steering. It struck the crash barrier, bounced off and spun. Without warning, it rolled, becoming an out-of-control mass of tangled metal, hurtling along the highway, shedding bits of itself and its human occupants.

The Chevy had used the time to edge its way alongside. Driving one-handed, Janek pulled out his autopistol. He triggered a rapid trio of shots into the pursuit car's passenger compartment, taking out the windows and sending hollowpoint slugs into the driver's body and head. The car slewed off course, striking the central barrier, and ground to a shuddering halt.

Janek brought them to a tire-burning stop, kicking open his door and exiting a fraction of a second after Cade.

Gunmen were erupting from the Chevy, their weapons up and firing.

Cade took one out with the SPAS, the force of the blast lifting the man off his feet and dumping him flat on his back, his chest a mass of pulsing red.

Ignoring the slugs chewing the concrete around him, Janek leveled his autopistol, aiming with deliberate precision before loosing off two shots that almost took his target's head clean off. The man went down hard, legs still kicking as he sprawled on the concrete.

The remaining gunman stood his ground with stoic indifference. Something about his manner told Cade he was a cyborg. The Justice marshal turned the full fury of the SPAS on the cyborg. His initial volley had little effect. The shot took away the robot's clothing and artificial skin, exposing the titanium-steel flexi-coat beneath. The cyborg rocked back on his heels but remained standing. He raised the subgun he carried and tracked in on Cade.

Janek took three long, agile steps. His left hand hit Cade between his shoulders, knocking him facedown on the ground. The autopistol in Janek's right hand was already lifting, lining up on the rogue cyborg's head. Almost without pause Janek triggered his weapon. The powerful slugs drilled in through the cyborg's eyes, coring deep into the electronic brain. The cyborg reacted instantly, losing all control of his actions and speech patterns. Spewing unintelligible sounds from his mouth, he ran back and forth across the road, arms and legs pumping frantically. Finally he ran into the crash barrier and hit the ground with a solid thump. His voice died to a soft whine, and he ceased moving.

Moving across to the cyborg, Janek stared down at the totalled machine. When he became aware of Cade standing in front of him he glanced up. "Hell of a thing to see," he said. "I've never witnessed a cybo die before."

Cade knelt beside the body. He pulled open the jacket, feeling in the pocket for any ID. He withdrew a badge that showed the cyborg to be Arnold Miles of the UCS. "What do you know," he muttered.

"Interesting," Janek said when Cade tossed the badge to him. "I suppose one of those others will be Feldstet."

Cade stood up. He caught the sound of approaching sirens. The police cruisers were on the way.

"Somebody is going to a lot of trouble to keep us from asking questions," Cade said. "I'd like to know who and why."

"Where do you want to start?"

"Let's get the formalities over with here," Cade said. "In the morning we check out the dead policemen's backgrounds. See what we can find out about them."

3

The apartment Cade shared with Janek was on the ninth floor of a thirty-year-old block on the West Side. On a good day Cade was able to see Central Park. That was when the smog decided to stay away. Air pollution still hadn't been defeated, and the city had bad days and worse days. That and the rain, and the sweltering summer heat, made living in New York less of an experience and more of a trauma.

Swinging the Ford off the street, Janek wheeled it down the ramp that led to the basement garage. He took the car to the far side of the dimly lit parking area, braking neatly inches from the scuffed concrete wall.

Cade left him to lock the car. He had the SPAS tucked under his arm. It was not a wise move to leave weapons in parked vehicles. There were a lot of people in need of guns in New York. Anyone who picked up a SPAS would have something he could make a good trade with.

Hitting the elevator button, Cade waited for the car to sink to the basement level. He stayed to one side of the doors, not wanting to present himself as an easy target in case someone came out shooting. It wasn't paranoia. Just simple day-to-day survival thinking.

The elevator doors slid open with a tired hiss. Cade stepped into the empty car, Janek coming up behind him. The cybo leaned across and thumbed the button for their floor. The car jerked, then began to rise. The metal walls of the car were dented and covered in multicolored graffiti.

Janek scanned the elaborate decorations, frowning and shaking his head with disapproval.

"I wish I could catch some of these so-called artists at work," he said.

"So you could arrest them?" Cade asked.

"So I could show them how to spell," the cyborg answered heatedly, stabbing a finger at the offending words. "Some of these creeps are real dunces."

"Your attitude problem is getting worse," Cade remarked with glee, pleased to see something getting a rise out of the usually calm Janek.

"Yeah?" Janek looked calm again and gave his lopsided shrug. "So sue me."

They stepped from the car on their floor and walked the corridor to the door of the apartment. Cade unlocked the door. He'd had the fancy ID-scanner lock removed because the damn thing kept refusing to admit him. Now he had a solid deadlock mechanism that would have defeated any of the local burglars. Armed with their computer-scan machines, they were left high and dry when confronted with an old-fashioned lock.

The apartment lights came on when Cade entered. He placed the SPAS in the closet just inside the door. Janek locked the door behind him.

"I suppose you want coffee?" he asked as he moved toward the kitchen.

"Only if it doesn't interfere with your social arrangements," Cade said.

He checked the vid-phone answering machine. Apart from the usual junk calls from various consumer agencies peddling everything from the latest-model cars to explicit offers from massage parlors, the only one that interested him was a short call from Kate Bannion.

Her face smiled at him from the screen, green eyes flashing with the sparkle that always left Cade with a knot in his stomach. Her rich red hair was tied up, drawing it back from her perfect oval face, with its high, sculptured cheeks and wide, sensuous mouth. Cade was always surprised at his reaction to her image. No matter how many times he saw her, he was left with the feeling he'd just been privileged to view something very special. In truth she *was* special to him. Cade had only known a few women intimately in his life. Since he'd met Kate, he realized he didn't need to know any others. Their relationship was both tender and tempestuous. He was stubborn and she was strong willed. She also had a sharp, inquisitive intellect that made her a match for any man. She used that keen brain in her job. Often too well, landing herself in enough trouble to keep Cade on the streets looking after her.

"Hi, T.J.," she said. "I won't be around for a few days. I'm taking off on a story. I have an interesting lead, and my source tells me this could be big. But I have to go undercover, so I'm dropping out of sight for a while. Just one more thing. If you spot me, don't let on. Okay? I'll make it up to you later. Promise."

Her image faded, followed by the message text that told him the call had been sent three days ago.

"That sounds like Kate's up to something risky. Don't you think, T.J.?"

Cade jumped and turned to glare at Janek, who was peering over his shoulder. "How many times do I have to tell you? Quit creeping up behind me like a damn housedroid."

"You know how to hurt a person's feelings," Janek said petulantly. "Do I look like one of those dusters on legs?"

"It could be arranged," Cade threatened.

"Here's your coffee," Janek said icily. He banged the mug down and stalked across the room. "I'll see you in the morning."

"Yeah," Cade muttered. He picked up the mug. "Hey, no staying up all night looking at those porndroid magazines."

The door closed with hard finality.

Cade crossed the living room and slumped on the couch. He picked up the remote and turned on the TV. He stared at the moving images on the screen. It was some old movie from the late 1990s. He realized he was watching the all-night movie channel. Idly he flicked through the stations, pausing when the screen showed a close-up of a pretty blond young woman writhing and moaning. He had stopped on one of the hard-porn satellite channels beamed in from Los Angeles, where the ever-powerful entertainment industry churned out its endless, colorful images. The Hollywood lobby, with its tenacious grip on local politics, had pushed through legislation five years back allowing it to transmit hard-core porn via the circling satellites. Even Washington Central had caved in. There was little point in making waves. Anything that might satisfy the nation's restless inhabitants, taking their minds off the coast-to-coast problems of twenty-first-century America, was welcome.

The blonde was acting out a sexual fantasy that left nothing to the imagination, but Cade wasn't interested. Kate Bannion was in the forefront of his thoughts. He flicked off the TV, then crossed to the window and stared out into the night. The darkness was pierced by many lights and interrupted at regular intervals by the drifting shapes of floating advertising drones. The silent craft, aglow with pulsing patterns of light and moving images, were a persistent and relentless homage to the consumer society that was still the driving force in the nation's economy.

Cade didn't see the neon messages. He was still emotionally occupied with Kate's call. He couldn't figure out why, but his instincts were telling him she could be mixed up in something he wouldn't like. Maybe it had been her reluctance to give him any details, the mystery she surrounded her vanishing act with. The thought tugged at Cade's patience until he turned sharply from the window.

He swore softly, but his exclamation merely compounded his frustration.

"You're worried about Kate, too?"

Janek was standing in the middle of the room. His hands were thrust deep in the pockets of his pants. At any other time Cade would have found the cyborg's stance amusing. Right now he was too concerned to even comment.

"She's up to something that could get her into a whole world of trouble."

Janek absorbed the expression, filing it away for future exploration.

"There should be someone at the newspaper office who knows what she's doing," he suggested.

Cade nodded. "I'll drop by there in the morning while you go and make some more inquiries about Feldstet and Miles. See if you can find anything on Connor. And try to dig up Bernie Stenner."

"Literally?" Janek asked.

"What?"

"T.J., I'm sure Stenner is dead. Digging him up could be messy."

"One day I'm going to find out just what they missed out when they put you together at Cybo Tech."

Janek didn't answer, but Cade could have sworn the cyborg had a smile curling the corners of his mouth when he walked off.

THE MORNING WAS thick and muggy. Dense clouds were forming off to the east, threatening rain for later in the day.

Cade paid the driver of the hovercab and stepped down to the landing pad that was situated on the upper-level mall of the *New York Century* communications building. The New York Century Tower rose ninety-five stories above Forty-second Street, close to the spot where the original *New York Times* building had been constructed back in 1904. The current tower housed newspaper and television offices, with vast studios and production facilities.

Crossing the concourse, Cade entered the covered ramp leading to the entrance. He ignored the hurrying crowd of employees as they made their way inside. At the high doors he was stopped by a securitydroid. The robot had piercing eyes and a mesh voice box. Its gleaming chrometal body blocked Cade's path.

"ID, please." The voice was basic and had a strong metallic twang.

Cade held up his badge so the droid could scan it. After a few seconds it stepped aside.

Cade went inside the building. The lobby was wide and airy. Soft music played in the background. He crossed to the information desk, where he was confronted by a cyborg receptionist. Cade had no problem recognizing a cyborg by now. Partnering Janek for so long had left him with an unerring instinct for picking them out of a crowd.

"May I help you, sir," the receptionist asked. She was attractive, with the kind of figure that couldn't be missed.

Cade showed his badge again, deciding that he might as well use his official clout to get him where he wanted to be.

"What can we do for you, Marshal Cade?"

"Kate Bannion works out of this building. I need some information about her."

The receptionist nodded. "We have received word that she's on an assignment at the moment, Marshal, and can't be reached."

"That's why I'm here. I need to talk with her immediate superior. Right now."

She picked up a vid-phone and punched in a number. When it connected, she spoke quickly but precisely. Leaning across the desk, Cade picked up the image of the man she was talking to and recognized him as Jerry Konsaki. He had met the man on a couple of occasions.

"I can find my way to Jerry's office," Cade said to the receptionist.

He made his way to the bank of elevators and stepped inside one. The skinny young man who operated the elevator glanced at Cade's badge and smiled nervously.

"You know Jerry Konsaki's floor?" Cade asked. The man nodded. "Take me there."

The elevator rose like a shuttle off the launching pad. Cade stepped out at the end of the journey, convinced he'd lost an inch in height. The elevator operator pointed along the shiny corridor.

"Sixth door along," he said.

Cade knocked on the door, but he didn't stand on ceremony. He went in right away.

Konsaki looked up with surprise, but when he saw who the visitor was he got up from behind his cluttered desk. He may have been installed in a building housing the latest technology, but his office resembled a paper-reclamation facility.

"Good to see you, T.J.," he said, reaching out to take Cade's hand.

"Jerry, I have to find out where Kate is. She could be in trouble."

"What makes you think that?"

"I got a message from her saying she's dropping out of sight on some story."

"That's right. You know Kate. She's never happy unless her assignments are the tough ones."

"Well, I have a gut feeling that this time she might have gone too far."

Konsaki frowned. He ran a lean, brown hand through his thinning hair. "I have to admit I've been spinning the worry beads myself since she left." He glanced at Cade. "She tell you what she was researching?"

Cade shook his head.

"She picked up a rumor about Darksiders going missing. Came to me all excited about it. Made me promise not to tell anyone until she'd had a chance to dig up some hard information...."

Konsaki caught the look that crossed Cade's face.

"You got something on this, T.J.?"

"A sniff is all. But the way things have been going, maybe it's more than just a rumor."

Gloomily Konsaki said, "And I let her go in by herself."

"Jerry, did she tell you who gave her the info?"

Konsaki's face betrayed his lack of knowledge. "Only thing I can tell you is she mentioned something about the old Link Tunnel."

Cade reached for the vid-phone. As he punched in the number, he hoped Janek had completed his digging and was back at the car.

4

Feldstet and Miles had been hanging out in a second-floor apartment in a crumbling building, situated off Third Avenue in East Harlem. The area, once the domain of New York's Hispanic population, who had christened it Spanish Harlem, or the Barrio, had undergone many changes. It still contained a mix of races. Massive financial and business infusions had attempted to change the grim facade of East Harlem but had failed to eradicate the hard core. The building Janek visited stood on the fringe of old East Harlem, not quite falling apart but beginning to sag around the edges.

He had parked the Ford and made his way inside. The apartment was still under police security. Janek flashed his badge, and the uniformed KC android patrolman opened the door for him.

Janek was out of the apartment within thirty minutes, confident it held nothing of interest to him. Apart from the expected, Janek failed to find anything to connect the UCS officers with any other organization or individual.

He stopped to ask the KC if there had been any visitors apart from the official police team.

"No, sir," the patrolman answered. "I've been here all the time. No callers at all."

Janek turned to leave.

As he did, he caught a flicker of movement at the far end of the corridor. It was caused by the curtain fluttering at the open window that allowed access to the fire escape.

"Have you seen anyone in the corridor since I went into the apartment?"

"No one."

Janek reached under his jacket for his handgun.

The window had been closed on his arrival. He'd scanned the corridor in both directions, and the window *had* been closed.

Touching the KC on the shoulder, Janek pulled out his heavy autopistol.

"We've got visitors now, patrolman."

A dark-clad figure stepped into view, leveling a rapid-fire combat rifle. The corridor echoed to the crash of autofire.

Janek felt something glance off his left arm, above the elbow. The impact caused him to pull his pistol off to the right, his first shot hitting the wall beyond the rifleman. With deliberate calmness he pulled the .44 autopistol back on track, triggering a succession of shots. The attacker took the entire volley in the chest. He was slammed back along the corridor, spewing blood from his body. He slithered along the wall, stumbling and falling, finishing the undignified journey with his face scuffing the rough carpet.

Next to Janek, the KC went down with two high-velocity slugs through his head. The android crashed to the floor, his service automatic still in its holster. He lay facedown, the fingers of one gloved hand working ceaselessly.

Beyond the angle of the corridor, where the landing opened out to the stairs, Janek picked up a scuffle of sound. He estimated there were two more of them. The metallic sound of weapons being racked came to his ears.

Taking long strides, Janek ran for the corner. As he reached it, a figure lunged into view. Sweeping up his left arm in a blur of movement, Janek let the back of his hand connect with the attacker's face. Bone crunched and bright blood sprayed in all directions. The injured man fell backward, coming up short against the railing at the head of the stairs. He had dropped the rifle he'd been carrying and now he fell to his knees, reaching for the weapon.

Close by, the third member of the group swung his own rifle around to bear down on Janek as the cybo burst into view. Janek's right arm arced around, finger pulling neatly against the .44's trigger. He put three hard shots into the man, blowing him across the landing and through the flimsy railing. With a shrill yelp the mortally wounded gunman fell from sight.

The one that Janek had hit in the face located his rifle. He made a grab for it, but Janek slammed his left foot down over the hand, pressing hard. Bones snapped audibly, and the man screamed. Janek reached down and hauled him to his feet. He swung the man around, crashing him bodily against the wall, then let him experience a jab with the .44.

"Okay, tough guy. Now we talk."

"Go fuck yourself, cop."

Janek rapped the barrel of the .44 against his cheek, just hard enough that it hurt.

"Wrong response. And a waste of effort in my case."

Janek held his gun to the man's head and pulled a pair of plasti-cuffs from his pocket.

"Assume the position," he snapped.

Once he had the man cuffed and secure, Janek put away his gun. He made the groaning perp walk ahead of him, down the stairs and out the building. Janek opened the Ford's rear door and shoved the guy inside. Then he reached for the handset of the car's radio. It buzzed just before he touched it.

Cade's voice rasped from the speaker.

"Let's get together for a meet," Cade said. "I think I've got something."

"I can better that," Janek replied. "I *do* have something. Two dead perps and one live one. They jumped me outside Feldstet and Miles's apartment."

"Get the sucker over to the office fast. He might have backup."

Janek didn't answer. His sensitive hearing had picked up the sound of an approaching vehicle, one that was moving far too fast to be driving normally, even in East Harlem.

"Janek?" Cade yelled through the speaker as he heard the cyborg mutter angrily.

Janek was too busy to reply. He'd spotted the black panel truck swinging in across the wide street. The side door slid open and armed figures leaned out. Heavy autoweapons opened up. A hail of slugs hammered the Ford, ripping through the door panels and shattering windows. Shredded upholstery filled the air.

Janek ran to the rear of the car as the panel truck swept by, his .44 blasting out shot after shot. He saw one of the gunners jerk back inside the panel truck, a burst of red marking the side of his skull.

Then the truck skidded in a tight circle, swaying as it came around. Janek watched it hurtle toward him. He stood his ground, pumping the rest of his clip at the windshield.

Someone opened up with an autoweapon again. The steady thump of large-caliber slugs rocked the Ford. Janek realized what they were a split second before the car exploded in a gush of flame.

Incendiary shells.

The missiles finally found the gas tank, and the riddled vehicle, along with Janek's prisoner, vanished in a roiling mass of red-orange flame. The fireball reached up and out, sending hungry tentacles of liquid heat over the immediate area.

Janek had turned to run but was caught by the blast. It picked him up and threw him bodily across the sidewalk. He was instantly engulfed in flames. His clothing and outer skin shriveled in the intense heat, leaving him a naked metal figure propped against the wall of the building. His titanium-steel casing smeared and sooty, Janek lay still and silent as the panel truck pulled away and raced off along the street.

5

Cade pushed through the swing doors of the Cybo Tech Corporation's New York facility, ignoring the protests of the administration clerk. The clerk was an android. It reached out to grasp Cade's sleeve.

"You can't just come in here without . . ."

Cade rounded on the clerk. There were no clothes to bunch in his fist, so he simply planted his big hand against the android's dull metal chest and shoved hard. The clerk backpedaled, then hit the wall with a metallic thud.

"Touch me again, and I'll pull your legs off!"

"Can I help you?" asked a soothing, well-modulated voice.

Cade spun on his heel, finding himself confronted by a tall, platinum blond female in a figure-hugging jumpsuit bearing the Cybo Tech logo. She was in her early thirties and strikingly attractive. She carried a clipboard in one hand.

"I'm Dr. Landers. I'm in charge here."

Cade showed her his badge. The blonde studied it closely, her expression remaining unchanged as she digested the information.

"So, Detective Cade, what can we do for you?"

"My partner was brought in a while ago. His name is Janek."

"Ah, yes, Detective Janek. He's in the operating room now."

"Is he going to be all right?" Cade demanded.

"That's what we're finding out right now, Detective Cade. Why don't you come with me and we'll take a look."

Dr. Landers turned on her heels and crossed the room. She had a trim figure beneath the jumpsuit. Following her, Cade found himself wondering whether she was a cyborg herself. His normal perception was a little befuddled at the present time, and he hadn't been able to decide on the doctor's status.

"In case you're wondering, I'm not a cybo," she said over her shoulder.

"But you are a mind reader?" Cade suggested.

Landers laughed softly, and slowing down, she fell in step beside Cade.

"Can I ask you something?"

"Go ahead."

"How long have you and Janek been partners?"

"Couple of years now. Why do you ask?"

"You display genuine concern. Almost as if Janek was human."

"Well, we work together. We share the same apartment. And we've been through some tough times together. Janek has pulled me out of some scary situations. I trust him with my life. That's the way a police partnership works."

"Interesting. Especially the way you refer to Janek."

They were making their way along a brightly lit corridor that was decorated in pale, soothing colors. It was hushed, but from somewhere up ahead they began to hear raised voices.

Cade recognized one of them. It belonged to Janek.

"Problems, doctor?" Cade asked innocently.

"Yes, and I think I know who's causing them."

The racket increased as they neared the operating room. A steady stream of arguments could be heard even though the doors were closed.

Dr. Landers pushed them open, striding into the chaos of the brightly lit operating room.

Banks of electrical equipment lined the walls. Computer consoles and monitor screens were ranged around the steel table where Janek lay. Electrodes were attached to his naked metallic torso. Cade felt oddly ill at ease seeing Janek in his exposed condition. He knew the cyborg as an efficient, complete individual—not as this gleaming, fleshless machine.

However, one thing hadn't changed. Janek's attitude, his desire to be on top of the situation. He had raised his voice, but it remained well modulated as he challenged the very presence of the Cybo techs gathered around him.

Janek was giving them a hard time, and the moment he spotted Cade, he decided he had an ally.

"T.J., get me out of here. These techs want to open me up. Tell them I'm just fine."

"Hey, take it easy, partner. Give them a break. They have a job to do."

"It's a waste of time," Janek snapped. "All I have is a headache and singed skin."

"Detective Janek, you have sustained shock trauma," Dr. Landers explained patiently. "You need a thorough examination in order to establish whether damage has occurred to any of your function-mode controls."

Janek pushed himself to a sitting position. His titanium skull reflected the overhead lights as he fixed Dr. Landers with a withering glance.

"I don't fancy anyone digging around inside my head. Just recycle my skin and let me out of here."

"Dr. Landers?" one of the O.R. staff queried. "Can we go ahead? It's difficult enough as it is."

"Up to now I've been reasonable with you people," Janek threatened. "That could change."

"Can I have a word, doctor?" Cade asked, touching Dr. Landers's arm.

Landers nodded, instructed the O.R. staff to wait, then followed Cade across the room. Her soft mouth had tightened in resignation.

"He needs attention," she insisted. "Look at his behavior."

They stood by one of the soundproof windows, looking out across the city. Rain drifted down from the lead gray sky.

"Doctor..." Cade said again, trying to gain her full attention.

"The Series 2000 is the most advanced cyborg ever produced. The merging of computer science and robotic evolution is the success of the century. Janek's brain is regarded as the ultimate in electronic intelligence. Despite that, Detective Janek is displaying attitudes unacceptable to Cybo Tech. The concussion from the explosion must have..."

"I think you've got it all wrong," Cade insisted. "Janek is always like this. It has nothing to do with the damn explosion. He was like this before that. Hell, he's been that way from the day I met him."

Landers glanced in the direction of the O.R. techs, who were standing in a loose group some distance away from Janek.

"You mean he's always been faulty? He has personality deficiencies?"

"No, doctor, I don't mean that."

"Then what do you mean, Detective Cade? I'd really like to know," Landers said wearily. "As far as I can see, we have a Series 2000 exhibiting extremes of behavior. He argues. There is definite antagonism toward authority. Janek also displays strong personal viewpoints on most matters. Detective Cade, in all my years with Cybo Tech I have never witnessed such behavior from a cyborg. Janek's departure from the structured personality is . . . is . . ." She paused, either unable or reluctant to use the right words.

Cade did it for her. "He acts like he was human. That what you were going to say?"

Landers stared at him as she fiddled with her clipboard absentmindedly.

"I have to admit that Janek does display certain human character traits."

"So why get hot about it? Janek was designed to have independent thought, to make his own decisions. The idea was to create a cybo as close as possible to us. Right? Well, congratulations, science has been successful."

Landers frowned. "Don't you ever get worried about him?" she asked. "Doesn't his behavior concern you?"

Cade grinned. "Hell, yes, but in most ways he is a lot more reliable than a human partner, although I don't think of him as being nonhuman. Janek's a pain in the butt a lot of the time. Comes from his curiosity. He needs to know. Always asking questions. It's weird sometimes. He knows a lot, but it isn't enough—he wants to know more about everything. He drives me crazy with his concern, fussing about my health, then the next minute he's getting steaming mad about something I said. And then there's this jazz thing. He's mad about jazz. Listens to it for hours. If we have a fallout, he doesn't sulk. He switches to some jazz channel and locks in. Can you figure it, doc? A cybo hot for jazz?

People who know him say he's crazy. Maybe he is. But that's part of the human condition, too! Character traits, you called it. Janek's an individual. He's changing. Developing. It's actually damn scary at times, come to think of it.

"But when it comes to the crunch, he's always there. When we get in a jam, I know I've got the best backup ever. I don't have to tell him what to do. He'll figure it out and be in the right place at the right time. Most days he's there before I am. And that's what counts on the street, a partner you know you can trust. So just give him his new skin, doctor, and let me worry about what goes on inside his head."

"Are you certain about this?" Landers asked as they moved back to where Janek sat.

"I'm the one who has to work with him," Cade said. "Do you think I'd carry on if I was worried?"

"I'm not sure I like it," Landers remarked.

"Optimum performance is the only thing that should count for you, doctor, and not whether you like something or not," Janek said with a superior air. "Now, give me some skin before I rust away in front of your eyes."

Landers shook her head. "On one condition, Detective Janek. You allow us to run a monitor check first. No interference. Just exterior checks of your vital functions. Then we put you through the regeneration unit."

"It's a deal," Janek agreed. He threw a hard glance in Cade's direction. "You were talking about me over there. Don't deny it, T.J. What were you saying?"

"In confidence, buddy," Cade said, grinning. "Can't repeat a word."

THE SYNTHETIC-SKIN regeneration process took a couple of hours. Cade used the time to make some calls.

He checked in with the Justice Department at Washington Central, requesting a computer search for any information on missing Darksiders. He received an answer after a couple of minutes. All the department could tell him was that they had been notified of some local rumors of Darksider disappearances in the New York area. No official investigation had been made at the time because the Urban Crime Squad had handled the matter locally.

Cade found that interesting. He took the last phrase to mean no investigation because it was being blocked somewhere in New York. The question was why?

Political expediency?

A lack of manpower? Or a lack of local interest?

Maybe someone was being protected.

Cade went for the last option, because there was already an interest in his investigation. Interest that wanted him to lay off.

There had already been two attempts to dissuade him and Janek from carrying on.

First the attack by Feldstet and Miles on Roosevelt Drive, then Janek's run-in with the hired guns.

Cade hadn't forgotten Feldstet and Miles's abduction of Bernie Stenner, or the fact that it had taken place in a very short time after his arrival at the local precinct house.

The facts behind Stenner's removal had been nagging at the back of Cade's mind for some time. Someone had tipped the UCS men about Stenner's arrest. For whatever reason, it had been deemed necessary to remove Stenner from the station. Most probably so that he would not divulge what he knew.

So who had informed Feldstet and Miles?

It had to be someone at the station.

Cade's initial contact had been with the pair of patrolmen who had arrived to take Stenner off his hands.

Treat and Dolan.

One, or both, could be on the payroll of the people responsible for the disappearance of the Darksiders. The way things were shaping up, maybe the whole damn NYPD was involved, Cade thought.

He spotted a vending machine in a corner of the waiting room and made a beeline to it. Feeding it money, he was delivered a plastic cup of indifferent coffee that did little to convince him of the outlandish claims the food industry made for having taken gigantic strides in improving convenience foods.

He glanced at his watch. Close to noon. Impatience was chafing at Cade's nerves. He'd been deliberately pushing the matter to the back of his mind, but during this period of inactivity, Kate Bannion's involvement with the missing Darksiders started to crowd him. He *was* concerned. Kate's impulsive nature could easily take her headfirst into something she might not be able to handle. The deeper Cade found himself drawn into the Darksider affair, the more he realized he was dealing with people who had no compunctions about murder. If they would try to take out a couple of police officers, they wouldn't hesitate when it came to an inquisitive news reporter.

The door opened, and Dr. Landers came into the waiting room. She gave Cade a tired smile. "He'll be through any minute. Just finishing getting dressed. He is complaining about the clothes you had delivered for him, something about the color scheme."

"Like I said, doctor, he hasn't changed. That guy is a pain."

She shook her head. "There you go again. You talk about him as if he was human."

"What else. I can't go around shouting *hey you*."

Dr. Landers handed Cade a small business card. "My number. Call me. I'd like to know more about Janek and how you two get on."

"Sure, doctor. I'll give you a blow-by-blow account."

The door swung open again, and Janek came into the room. He was fully dressed and back to his normal appearance. Even down to the disapproving scowl on his face.

"T.J., your taste in clothing lacks a certain, er, refinement. I look like a funeral director at a rained-out burial."

"You got me there, partner," Cade said. "Dr. Landers, thanks for your help."

"My pleasure."

Janek ran a hand over his new skin. "Nice work, doctor. Thank you," he said, and followed Cade out the door.

"Where to, T.J.?"

"The department office," Cade said. "Time for you to talk to some of your computer buddies."

They picked up an aircab outside the Cybo Tech building. It swept out across the rain-streaked canyons of the city, silently gliding between the soaring skyscrapers and elevated roads, heading down toward the Civic Center, where the Justice Department had its New York headquarters. The original site of the Civic Center had been redesigned five years previously and a new, fourteen-story structure erected where the old Federal Building had stood. The Justice Department had the top six floors of the building.

The cab dropped Cade and Janek on the rooftop pad. They made their way to the elevator bank and took the car that was available only for Justice Department officials. The car dropped to the twelfth floor, the doors sliding open to admit them to the humidified atmosphere of the department.

"What do you want me to look for?" Janek asked as he followed Cade into their office.

"I want a tie between Treat or Dolan and whoever is running this Darksider deal," Cade said.

"Because they were the only ones to be in contact with Stenner before Feldstet and Miles showed up?" Janek said.

"Yeah. The time period is too damn small for anyone else to have been involved. The way the desk sergeant acted at the precinct cuts him out, and the place is too busy for anyone else to take much notice of such a small-time crook." Cade dropped into his swivel chair. "I'm going on instinct, Janek. Let's try for a connection between the two patrolmen and whoever is footing the payroll."

"What are you going to do?"

"Me?" Cade grinned. "I'm putting my feet up and taking it easy."

"Typical," Janek muttered as he headed for the side office and his computers. "I thought we had a fifty-fifty partnership going here."

"Hey, did I tell you that?"

Janek glanced over his shoulder. "You know damn well you did."

"Looks like I told another lie," Cade said.

Janek settled down at his computer banks, making a fingertip electronic link with the machines.

Still smiling, Cade fished a pack of cigars from his desk and lit one. He turned to the computer unit on his own desk and switched it on. He called up the New York directory, tapping into the display for the underground tunnel systems. He sat and scanned the complex maze of subway tunnels, service and access tunnels, the abandoned networks, the different levels that lay deep beneath the city. The folklore of the tunnels and the people said to inhabit them went back years, well into the previous century. The legends had been created, retold and elaborated over the decades, until no one knew the truth anymore. But there was one undeniable truth. Thousands *did* live beneath the city. They were born, existed and died there. Some, who lived at the lowest levels, never saw the light of day. They lived in near darkness, away from the sunlight. They were able to see in the dark, it was said. If they were brought into the open, they would cower in terror, begging to be returned to their shadow world.

The Darksiders were shunned by the rest of society. No one bothered about them one way or another. The underground dwellers didn't intrude on daily life, so they were left alone. Ignored. Forgotten by most.

But suddenly they were Cade's problem because there appeared to be some kind of unusual criminal activity—aside from the standard stuff—going on that involved the Darksiders. There had already been deaths and attempted murder—and Cade had a personal stake in the matter now.

Kate Bannion.

He was still staring at the monitor when Janek came back into the office. He stood in front of Cade's desk, holding a computer printout in his hand.

"I think we have our connection, T.J.," he said.

Cade took the sheet and scanned the mass of printed information. "Tell me in simple words," Cade said.

"The information on Dolan is very interesting. He's the same rank as his partner, so that means he's on the same salary. However, when I accessed his bank account, the computer asked me which one. It appears our friend Dolan has a second account. Different bank in another part of the state. This one has quite substantial amounts of money in it. He opened it a couple of years ago and has been depositing cash payments on a regular basis ever since.''

"Looks like Officer Dolan has been a busy boy," Cade said.

"Not too smart, though," Janek said. "He did open a second account out of town, but he still used his own name and address."

"Dolan's greedy, but he's obviously a guy with limited intelligence. Probably figured a bank out of town would be safe, but he didn't have the imagination to give himself an alias. What does that tell you about a law-enforcement officer who deals with criminals in his work?"

"He hasn't learned very much," Janek said, "or maybe he learned not to trust anyone. Keeping the second account in his name makes it easier to get at. You don't have to go to the extremes of dreaming up a new identity."

"We can ask him when we drop by to see him," Cade said.

"I made a check, and he's off duty today. He lives on the West Side, just off Columbus Avenue. Apartment D2, third floor."

Cade bounded to his feet and snatched up his jacket. "Let's go check out a new car and take a ride."

6

They saw the police air cruisers before they reached Dolan's apartment building. There were street cruisers parked outside the building, and a barrier already locked off the entrance.

A uniformed officer halted their car. Janek showed his badge as he and Cade climbed out, pulling on waterproof coats against the rain that was still falling.

"You got an interest in this?" the officer asked.

"If it's to do with Officer Dolan, we have," Cade said.

"Looks like you're too late," the patrolman said. "We got the call because somebody heard shooting. By the time we responded, it was all over."

"Dead?" Janek asked.

"Wouldn't you be with a full clip of .44 slugs in you? Somebody really wanted Dolan dead." The officer's voice was taut with anger, and both Cade and Janek knew that there would be a lot of anger expressed over Dolan's death. It was a case of one of their own being murdered. Cade figured he'd keep his suspicions about Dolan's illegal dealings to himself at that point.

Janek nudged his elbow. "No point in mentioning Dolan's extra pay is there, T.J.?" he said softly, anticipating Cade's thoughts.

"No. We'll keep that between you and me for the time being."

A plainclothes detective came out of the building. Stocky and bullnecked, he pushed his way through the barrier,

snapping orders to the assembled officers. He spotted Cade
and Janek and crossed to meet them, pulling up the collar
of his crumpled topcoat. Cade had known him for a long
time, and he maintained a sparring relationship with the
man.

"Hey there, T.J. How's it rolling for you?"

"Fine, Milt."

Milt Schuberg glanced at Janek. "See you still got the tin
man partnering you. Don't you ever get tired of having the
damn thing trailing around in your shadow?"

"Janek and me get along just great, Milt."

"Fucked if I can understand wanting a tin man for a
backup. What's wrong with a real partner?"

"You can't switch them off when they talk too much,"
Cade said dryly. "Now, what have you got on Dolan's
murder?"

"Who said it was murder?" Schuberg asked defiantly.

"It sure as hell isn't suicide, Milt."

"Yeah, well, we don't have too much yet. Whoever did it
just kicked his door off its hinges and went in blasting. Shot
Dolan so full of holes he just about leaked all his blood over
the carpet."

"Did anyone see or hear anything concerning the perp?"
Janek asked.

Schuberg looked up at the cyborg. When he spoke, his
voice had lost its normal tone. He spoke to Janek as if he
were addressing a pet animal.

"Why, yes. One man in the street saw him running out.
The bad guy got in a panel truck and it went down the street.
That way. Very fast. You get all that?"

Janek nodded. "I got it," he said. "And I'm pleased
you're at least trying to overcome that annoying speech im-

pediment, Detective Schuberg. T.J., I'll go and talk to the witness."

As Janek walked off, Schuberg rounded on Cade. "You let him speak like that to people? Son of a bitch wants his ass kicked! Stupid tin freak."

"Seems to me you asked for it. Why don't you quit this thing you've got against cybos?"

"Say what you like, T.J. I just don't feel right with 'em around."

"Yeah? Well, that's your problem. Mine's checking out Dolan's murder."

"Why is the Justice Department interested in a NYPD cop getting blown away?"

"It's against the law, Milt. Surely even you know that," Cade replied, and left it at that.

"So you are going to play clam." Schuberg's tone changed. "I got a right to know, T.J."

"Only if I decide you have."

"T.J., I can take this higher," Schuberg said, waving a thick finger at Cade.

"I don't have time to argue, Milt." Cade turned away and crossed to where Janek was completing his questioning of the witness. "Anything?"

Janek nodded for Cade's benefit, then dismissed the witness. "Thank you for your cooperation, sir."

Returning to their car, Janek waited until they were out of earshot of the local police, and especially Schuberg, who was staring in their direction.

"The killer ran out of the building, still carrying his gun. I guess he figured it would keep people away. A panel truck was waiting for him. It was painted black, T.J., and had a starred windshield."

"The truck you encountered was black," Cade said. "And you laid a few shots into the windshield."

"Our witness managed to recall some of the numbers on the license plate. They tallied with the ones I recorded."

"I didn't get time to ask before, but did you run a check on it back at the office?"

Janek smiled thinly. "The panel truck is registered to a freight company in Newark."

"You got a look at the perps you tangled with. Did your witness ID the guy who ran out of Dolan's building?"

"Yes. His description was sketchy, but it matched one of the gunmen at the Feldstet and Miles building."

"Enough for you to run a computer match?"

"I believe so."

Schuberg caught up with them as they reached the car.

"Gimme a break, T.J.," he said. "You know how jumpy everybody gets when one of our own is killed. You got anything?"

Cade shook his head. "Only a description of the perp. Your boys will already have that. We'll run it through our computer and see if anything shows. If it does, I'll give you a call."

"Okay," Schuberg said. He looked cold and wet and none too happy.

"I'm sorry about Officer Dolan," Janek said.

"Yeah, thanks," Schuberg replied without realizing who he was talking to.

"Milt, as a matter of interest," Cade said. "What do you know about Connor? Captain over at UCS."

"I know enough to stay away from the mother. Word of warning, T.J., if you get mixed up with Connor, watch your back. He's a hard one. I've heard it rumored he's not too straight, either, but no one has the guts to say it to his face. UCS is a tough outfit."

Schuberg's craggy face froze. He stared at Cade for a moment, then gave a thin smirk.

"You son of a bitch," he said. "I heard that a couple of UCS men got downed. You know something about that? What's going on, T.J.? It got anything to do with Dolan?"

"Right now, Milt, I'm not sure. And that is the truth."

"Christ, T.J., Connor's going to be after your hide. You watch it, buddy, and I mean that."

"I'll be in touch," Cade said, then reached for the cruiser's door and slipped behind the wheel. He fired the engine and took off with a screech of tires.

"Isn't it time you took a refresher course for driving?" Janek asked as he strapped himself in. "You tend to be irresponsible behind the wheel of a car."

"Me? Irresponsible? Janek, you've got a nerve."

"Only humans have nerves. That's why they're so touchy. Makes them bad tempered, as well."

Janek slumped back in his seat, eyes half-closed, and Cade knew he'd called up his jazz circuit. The cyborg's lips curved in a satisfied smile, his head moving slightly as he lost himself in the rhythm of a tune Cade couldn't even hear.

Cade petulantly fished out a cigar. He fired it up and deliberately blew a cloud of smoke in Janek's direction. He saw his partner's nose twitch as he inhaled the aroma, but even that failed to intrude on his relaxed condition.

In retribution Cade stomped hard on the gas pedal, sending the car speeding back downtown, the siren screaming to clear a way. As he weaved in and out of the traffic, the cruiser wreathed in a permanent mist of spray from the wet street, Cade noticed with triumph that Janek's right hand was gripping the edge of his seat. If it had been possible, Janek's knuckles would have turned white.

IT TOOK JANEK exactly eight minutes to come up with an ID picture of the suspect. He fed his stored image of the perp directly into the office computer, linked to the national information bank in Washington Central. The network's data store digested the computer directives and matched it to Washington's files.

"Jak Regis. Forty-five years old. Local hardcase. Spent most of his teen years on correction farms. Graduated to violent crime once he got himself established in New York. Built himself a rep as a gunhand. Linked to a number of killings but never indicted. He has powerful friends, T.J. Whenever he's been picked up for questioning, there has always been a lawyer around to bail him out. None of his arrests have ever reached court."

"Who represents him?" Cade asked.

"A lawyer called Lippin."

"Max Lippin?" Cade asked, and when Janek nodded, he said, "There's something fishy here, Janek. Max Lippin is strictly skidsville. The guy's so dumb he can hardly write his own name. If he's working bail for Regis, then he's fronting for someone higher up. No way Max Lippin is playing solo. That little shyster is operating out of his league."

The vid-phone burst into life. Cade snatched up the handset and watched the angry face of Captain Connor emerge from the static.

"What the fuck is going on, Cade? I've been trying to get in contact all damn day. Where the hell do you Justice jockeys hide out?"

"It's a busy life, Connor. Right now I'm even busier, so what do you want?"

"Don't play dumb-ass with me, buster. Last night you killed one of my men and totalled a cybo."

"You forgot to mention the gunhands your boy had with him," Cade said. "And the fact they tried to blow me off the highway."

"That's what *you* say, Cade," Connor yelled. "But they can't speak for themselves. Look, mister, I don't give a shit who you work for. Leave my people alone."

"Connor, I told you last night, and I'll tell you again. My prisoner was taken away by your people. An unauthorized removal and you know it, so don't play the bullyboy with me. You might scare the local cops, but it won't work with me. I'm still digging into this mess, Connor. If I find anything that suggests you're less than lily-white, I'll be calling in at your office. Now, chew on that, Captain."

Cade slammed the phone down, grabbed his jacket and headed for the door. "Let's go," he said to Janek. "If we move fast, we can pick Lippin up at his favorite afternoon haunt."

The rain still sluiced down out of a darkening sky as Cade rolled the cruiser to a stop at the curb. They were in the dingy streets behind Times Square. Here, away from the main drag, were the strip joints and massage parlors. Shabby theaters proclaimed the best porn movies in town. Holographic images of naked couples enticed the customers through the doors. The narrow streets were littered with trash and abandoned cars. Streetwalkers wandered back and forth, their painted faces and vacant eyes revealing the hopelessness of their lives.

"Why doesn't the city do something about places like this, T.J.?" Janek asked.

"Costs money, partner, and the city council hasn't been able to balance the books for years. Come on, Janek, you've studied New York's social history. The city's made a career out of going bankrupt.''

They pushed past the shambling derelicts and raucous prostitutes, then Cade turned in at the entrance to a garish theater.

"We're going in here?" Janek asked.

"Maybe you're too young and sensitive for this," Cade said.

"Don't bet on it."

The big man at the door blocked their way.

"You didn't pay," he growled. He was over six feet tall and almost as wide. His near-bald skull seemed to protrude over his small, cold eyes as he hunched forward.

"Janek, explain," Cade said. He wasn't in the mood to argue with the guy, so he took the easy option.

Janek said, "We're justice marshals, and we need to take a look inside."

The doorman grinned, showing a set of gleaming synthetic teeth. "You want to get your rocks off, you pay like everyone else."

Janek smiled thinly. "T.J., where do they come up with these throwbacks?"

The doorman's brain lurched into first gear, and he scowled at Janek.

"Who you callin' a throwback?"

He launched a massive fist in Janek's direction. The cyborg leaned swiftly back out of harm's way. As the doorman was pulled in toward him by the force of the punch, Janek's right hand flashed up and forward, catching the man's wrist. He increased the pressure, his titanium fingers cutting off circulation and numbing the nerves. His other hand caught hold of the doorman's left thigh. Janek raised him off the floor, turned effortlessly and threw the man into the corner of the foyer.

"If you're still around when we come out," Janek said, "I'll show you my other trick."

The auditorium had rings of seats set around the ten-foot raised platform on which the holographic porn movie was playing. The life-size images of two men and three girls relentlessly performed a variety of sexual acts on a king-size bed. The images were as clear as if they were being enacted by live performers. The men were in perfect physical condition and possessed the obligatory oversize sexual organs, while the females had fantasy figures, complete with superb breasts and supple limbs.

As Janek followed Cade into the semidarkness, he tapped his partner on the shoulder.

"Are these images supposed to represent human form at its best?"

"In a way," Cade said, not sure where Janek's line of questioning would lead. "Why?"

"I can equate the females with Kate," Janek said tactfully. "But the males, well, they seem to be somewhat different, especially when it comes to a certain part of the anatomy."

Cade pretended not to hear. He hadn't expected Janek to bring up that particular incident at a time like this.

The cyborg had wandered into Cade's bedroom during one of Kate's visits and stood watching with almost childlike interest. It had been Kate, glancing over Cade's shoulder, who had seen Janek watching. To her credit she hadn't panicked but simply tapped Cade's naked back.

"What?" he'd asked rather absentmindedly. Being interrupted at such a crucial moment hadn't caught him at his most receptive.

"We have a visitor," Kate had managed to say before exploding with laughter.

Forgetting for the moment his vulnerable state, Cade had twisted his head around to see Janek standing there.

"Goddamn it, Janek! What?" he had yelled, Kate's laughter only feeding his anger.

"I heard strange noises. I thought someone was having a problem."

Kate had collapsed beside Cade, hysterical with laughter.

"T.J., what were you doing to Kate?"

Through her laughter Kate had asked, "Yes, what were you doing to Kate?"

Cade had scowled at her, not trusting himself to speak. His anger was rising as swiftly as his passion wilted, and was compounded when he realized that Janek was watching his physical reaction closely.

"Why is it doing that, T.J.?" the cyborg had asked, switching his gaze to Cade's taut features.

The final question had been too much for Kate. Burying her face in the pillow, she had been reduced to uncontrollable laughter, tears streaming down her beautiful face, the sleek curves of her shapely body quivering in spasms.

Cade was able to laugh about the incident himself later, but he had always kept the bedroom door locked from that day on.

They spotted Max Lippin near the front, relaxing in one of the body-molding recliner seats provided for the paying customers. He was so engrossed in the movie that he didn't notice Cade standing over him. Not until Cade leaned over and tapped his shoulder.

"Max, I hate to disturb you when you're working, but we need to talk."

Lippin twisted his head around, peering up at Cade. His thin features wrinkled into an expression of annoyance, and he waved a bony hand at Cade.

"I have nothing to say to you, Cade."

"Wrong answer, Max."

Cade caught hold of Lippin's jacket and hauled him out of the recliner. He dragged the protesting man out of the auditorium, through the foyer and out onto the street. Janek had moved ahead of them. He opened the cruiser's rear door. Cade shoved Lippin inside, then followed. Janek slammed the door shut and moved around to slip behind the wheel. "Where to?" he asked as he fired up the engine.

"Just cruise," Cade said. "Stay off the main drag. I don't want too many witnesses."

Lippin gave a strangled cry, his lean body wriggling across the rear seat. He tried to open the door of the cruiser as Janek pulled away.

"Take it easy, Max. You act like a man with something to hide," Cade said. "You got something to hide? That it, Max?"

Lippin turned suddenly, defiance sharpening his feral eyes. He sat upright, brushing at the lines of his flashy suit.

"What's this all about, Cade?"

"It's about a cheap little lawyer trying to make the big time, Max."

"I don't have time to play games. What do you want?"

"Answers, Max. Like who pays Jak Regis's bail every time you spring him? Who sets up the deals? I know it isn't you. You don't handle people like Regis. So who is pulling the strings for you?"

"What the hell, Cade, you jealous because I raised my game? Can't a guy improve himself?"

Cade even grinned at that, because it proved his suspicions. "Max, I don't gave a damn how high you go. But don't think you're taking me in. You're fronting for someone. Now give, or I'll have Janek run us down by the East River so I can dump you."

Lippin gave a halfhearted laugh. The sound died in his throat as he caught the expression in Cade's eyes. Whatever else he might have thought about the Justice marshal, Lippin knew that T.J. Cade was not a man who threatened lightly. He also knew that for somebody of Cade's caliber, working for the Justice Department meant that he had a free hand when it came to settling his cases.

"Jesus, Cade, what do you want from a guy? All I do is a little representing for a client. There a law against it?"

"If you've nothing to hide, Max, why get in such a state about it?"

"The client wanted confidentiality is all."

Lippin leaned forward in his seat. He rubbed a hand across his face. The pale flesh was moist.

"Is it hot or not? Hey, you got the heater on or something?" he called to Janek.

"Calm down, Max," Cade suggested. "Just give me what I need."

"Yeah, sure. Look, I take on assignments for this guy. He calls and gives me instructions. I do the business and he pays me."

"This guy got a name?"

"Hamilton Lasall. Has his own law firm."

Janek's head inclined slightly as he picked up the name. It would be filed away inside his skull for checking when he and Cade returned to the office.

"That it, Max?"

Lippin nodded vigorously. "I don't know who employs Lasall, and that's the truth. They don't say, I don't ask."

"Stop the car, Janek," Cade said.

Lippin glanced at the Justice cop. "That it? I can go?"

"Sure, Max. Like I said, all I wanted was a couple of answers."

Lippin climbed out of the cruiser, still watching Cade. It was as if he expected Cade to suddenly reach out and shoot him. Once the lawyer was on the sidewalk, Cade told Janek to drive on.

"T.J., he'll be on the phone by now, telling his client we've been questioning him."

"Sure he will," Cade said, grinning expansively.

"Which is what you want him to do?"

"I want him to pass the word that we're still digging. It helps if you keep everyone guessing."

"The principle being that when people become upset they do unexpected things?"

"You got it."

"Back to the office?" Janek asked.

"Right. Let's run some checks on Lasall. In the morning we go and see what the Darksiders have to say."

"What about Regis?"

Cade grunted to himself.

"What does that mean?" Janek asked.

"I have a feeling Regis will show up again sooner or later."

7

The transit authority officer wasn't too happy having to guide Cade and Janek to the junction with the main tunnel. As he led them along the access tunnel, he made constant references to the dangers of the place. His grumbling seemed endless.

Janek finally got tired of the man's whining. He moved up beside their guide and caught his attention.

"What?" the man asked irritably.

"You want to make me happy?"

"Huh?"

"Just show us the damn way and quit giving us a hard time. Okay? If you have to grumble, mime it."

The man began to protest, then thought better of it when he took a good look at Janek's height. He hunched his shoulders and stomped forward.

"T.J., are we going to find anything down here?" Janek asked.

"Right now I don't even know what we're supposed to be looking for," Cade admitted. "All we have are rumors of Darksiders missing and Kate wandering around down here."

"I don't think it was one of her better ideas."

"You and me both, partner."

Minutes later the officer halted. He beckoned Cade and Janek forward, indicating the way ahead with his flashlight.

"About thirty yards on you'll hit the down-ramp that merges with the main tunnel. We've spotted Darksiders around the area for years."

"You sure this is where the girl went in?" Cade asked, referring to Kate.

"Hell, sure. I won't forget her in a hurry. You know, all that red hair and the body inside that jumpsuit. I can feel my dick wakin' up just thinking about her."

Janek's right hand snaked out to grasp Cade's arm as he began to move forward. Only the shadowed gloom of the tunnel hid Cade's angry expression. The cyborg held his partner immobile until the transit cop had walked ahead of them and was out of earshot.

"Easy, T.J.," Janek whispered.

Just then, their guide decided that he'd taken them far enough and that his part of the job was over. He turned back, ready to make his way out again.

"Glad I'm not the one going in there," he stated. The easy grin on his lips failed to soften the hard gleam in his eyes. "But, hell, it's what they pay you guys for, isn't it?"

He began to retrace his footsteps back along the access tunnel, leaving Cade and Janek on their own.

Cade led the way forward, down the ramp to where the access tunnel joined with the abandoned subway tunnel. This section of the system had been closed ten years earlier, making way for the improved rapid-transit system that now ran through its own new tunnel. Every few minutes the subdued sound of the trains could be heard through the walls of the old tunnel. Scattered litter was strewn across the ramp. There was more filth on the floor of the main tunnel. Most of it was the accumulated trash that marked years of human presence and dwelling. From rotting food to old TV sets, broken furniture and automobile tires. The walls and curving top of the tunnel were streaked with black soot from the countless fires that had been lit over the years to provide the means for cooking or simply for warmth.

There was an all-pervading smell lingering in the air. A cloying, disturbing odor, it was a mix of spoiling food and human waste, of damp and fetid air. It spoke of decay and death, and the impermanence of man and his society.

"How the hell are you supposed to get used to this stench?" Cade grumbled.

"Does it bother you, T.J.?"

"Damn right it does," Cade said. "You're lucky you can't smell it."

"I *can* smell it, only I react in a different way." Janek smiled indulgently. "If you think about it, T.J., I'm pretty well superior to you in a number of ways. I don't get sick. I don't need to eat or drink. Drugs don't interest me, and I haven't got your desperate need for sex."

"And you figure that makes you superior?"

"Don't you?"

"You've just made me realize my entire existence is a total waste," Cade said.

"I didn't mean to upset you, Thomas."

"Don't worry about it. I'll try to bear the mental scars."

They progressed along the tunnel, scattering debris as they walked and disturbing the rats that infested the area.

"Don't you like them?" Janek asked, watching his partner's reaction to the rodents.

Cade took a wild kick at a particularly large rat that stood its ground as he approached. The rat squealed angrily, darting at Cade, who stumbled back.

With unerring accuracy Janek turned and lashed out with his foot. The toe of his boot lifted the rat and flung it yards back along the tunnel. It thudded to the ground and scurried off into the darkness.

As he rejoined Cade, Janek raised his head, peering into the darkness that lay ahead of them.

"Someone there," he said to Cade. "More than one. Could be six, maybe seven people."

Janek's vision was equipped with the ability to magnify distant objects. He was also able to utilize any source of light to enhance his night-vision capability.

Cade eased his .357 from its holster, dropping his hand to his side, the concealed weapon hidden from sight but readily accessible. He continued moving forward, aware of Janek to his left. He concentrated on his own approach, safe in the knowledge that the cyborg would be on instant response if trouble showed.

The group of figures slipped from the gloom, forming into recognizable shapes. Janek had been right. Cade counted six of them. They were clad in the raggedy dress that seemed part of the Darksider mystique. An odd mix of current fashions curiously blended with garments that had a distinctly medieval look to them. Leather and wool mixtures that were direct opposites to synthetic fibers, yet seemed to mate with them.

As the Darksiders drew closer, Cade picked out individual faces, noting that they all had the same dead white complexions. Years of existing below ground, away from the sun and air, had turned their skins pale, giving them an almost ghoulish appearance.

The leader of the Darksiders brought his group to a stop. He was a tall, round-shouldered man, his stringy, graying hair falling in tails around his pinched features. Dark eyes looked Cade over with unconcealed hostility.

"What do you want down here?" he demanded. His voice had a hollow ring to it. "You don't belong."

"And you don't own this place," Cade reminded him. "So let's get off that track right away."

"Maybe you should count how many there are of us."

Cade sighed. Another hardcase.

"Don't play games unless you know the rules," he said, and eased the autopistol so it could be seen. "My name's Cade. This is Janek, my partner. We're from the Justice Department. Only reason we're down here is to look into rumors of Darksiders going missing. There any truth in that?"

"We don't need your fuckin' help," a voice yelled from the back of the group.

"Nobody gives a damn about us normally. Why all the fuss now?"

"Because if a crime's been committed, it's my job to deal with it. Darksiders or bankers, makes no difference to me. I treat everyone the same."

The Darksider leader stepped forward, his face taut with anger. "I don't believe you," he said.

"And just who are you, mister? Somebody special or just a loose mouth?"

"They call me Rolf. I speak for these people."

"Well, I don't give a damn what you believe, Rolf," Cade told him. "If there's something going on, I need to know about it. I only learned about this two days ago, and since then people have been trying to kill me every time I bring the subject up. When that happens, it gets personal."

Cade noticed other figures edging out of the shadows, expanding the crowd, which now included women and children.

"I didn't come down here to admire the view or to hassle you people. Believe me, I'd rather be up top. So tell me what's going down."

Rolf refused to give in. He remained silent, staring with his empty eyes at Cade and Janek.

"Damn you, Rolf!"

The shout came from somewhere in the crowd of Darksiders. It was the determined voice of a young woman. She pushed her way through the crowd, a slim, pale figure, then elbowed her way past Rolf.

"He won't help you. He never does," she said spiritedly. "If he'd lost someone, it might be different. But he doesn't have anyone to lose, so he makes us all suffer by refusing help."

"What do we call you?" Cade asked.

"I'm Lisa."

"Have you lost someone, Lisa?" Janek asked.

She nodded.

"My man. They took him three weeks ago. During one of their raids. They took over a hundred that night. We don't know what's happened to them, but I believe they're all dead. I don't believe we'll see any of them again. I said the same to that journalist after she agreed to come down and help us."

Lisa turned on the man named Rolf, and the anger pitched her voice higher. "She came to help, but he turned against her. Made things difficult."

"She was an outsider," Rolf snapped back. "What good are outsiders? She wanted us to resist."

"At least it's doing something," Lisa said. "You let them come and do nothing. We've lost too many people to allow it to go on. Maybe it's time we asked why you let them take our people."

"Yes," someone yelled. "Make him tell."

"Maybe he's in with them," another suggested.

"Speak up, Rolf, we've a right to know what's going on."

"Looks like the ball's in your court, Rolf," Cade said.

Rolf flicked his hand, and two of the men close by him began to open their coats.

Oh, hell! Cade thought as he caught the soft glint of metal. The mothers are armed!

That was unusual for the Darksiders, who didn't believe in weapons of violence. Their very retreat beneath the ground was partly due to their desire to stay away from the mad struggle overhead in the city, a struggle that some of them were not equipped to handle, while others refused to take part in the daily scramble.

Rolf, it appeared, lived by a different set of rules.

There was no time to warn anyone to get out of the way. The action had started, and there was no way to stop it going through its deadly cycle.

Cade dropped to one knee, swinging up the .357 in a single movement, tracking in on the guy closest to him. He saw the ugly snout of a sawed-off shotgun—an ideal combat weapon in the close confines of the tunnel—and reacted instinctively. The autopistol crackled with fire, Cade triggering fast and accurately. His bullets ripped into his target's chest, picking him up and driving him backward before dumping him in a bloody, squirming heap on the floor of the tunnel.

Beside him Janek had tracked in on his adversary, his weapon up and firing before the guy could clear his own scattergun from his clothing. Janek's bullets drove deep into his torso, gouging slivers of wood from the shotgun's stock as they peppered his body. He twisted around, screaming, blood erupting from his tattered clothing, and crashed face-first into the curving tunnel side.

In the seconds given to him by his dying accomplices, Rolf managed to pull out his own handgun. It was a large laser-sighted Beretta .44, one of the newer versions of the weapon. He turned, waving the gun as he tried to lose himself in the crowd. They scattered before him, panic lending strength to their limbs.

Rolf reached out and grabbed a teenage girl by the loose front of her tunic. He swung her around to cover his front, his arm pulled tight against the girl's throat. The Darksider jammed the muzzle of his weapon against the side of the trembling girl's head. Despite the glittering fear in her eyes, she managed to remain silent, offering no resistance.

"You want this bitch dead?" Rolf yelled. "Then try and stop me. I'll kill her."

Janek waved Cade back, moving to the side of the tunnel where he merged with the deep shadows, out of Rolf's sight. Cade remained where he was, the autopistol sagging in his fist. He let Janek make the play, accepting that the cyborg's superior skills were the only ones capable of putting an end to Rolf's dangerous game.

Rolf had cleared the fringes of the crowd and was fast vanishing in the darkness farther down the tunnel. He kept the muzzle of his pistol pressed to his hostage's skull.

"Nobody follows me," he warned. "First one I see move, I'll blow her brains all over the goddamn tun—"

He never completed the word. There was a single shot, coming from the darkness off to his right. The bullet cored through his skull, burning deep into his brain before blowing his head wide open. As Rolf arced backward, he lost his grip on the girl, who immediately dropped to her knees. The Darksider's gun hand jerked up in the air, finger pulling back on the trigger. His bullet whacked into the tunnel roof, splintering tiles. Rolf's body hit the floor, kicking and jerking away his final moments in silent agony.

Cade moved to stand over the Darksider. Rolf's gun lay on the ground close by the twitching fingers of his right hand. Cade kicked the weapon clear, then crouched beside Rolf. He ignored the bloody wreckage of the man's head as he made a thorough search of Rolf's clothing. There was a thin wallet tucked inside the man's wide belt. Flicking through it, Cade found more than three thousand dollars in cash and a credit chip. There were a couple of vid-phone cards. They were preprogrammed cards, with the number already coded in, so the caller didn't need to know the number he was calling. Once in the vid-phone slot, the card fed the number sequence to the machine and placed the charge for the call to the owner of the number.

"Run a check on these when we get back to the office," Cade said as Janek appeared at his side. "And the credit chip."

"What was Rolf doing with a credit chip?" asked the young woman who had forced the game to its abrupt conclusion. "Darksiders don't have credit chips. Or guns."

"I'd say, Lisa, that Rolf was probably working with the people who've been kidnapping Darksiders," Janek observed.

"Bastard!" Lisa said angrily. "He sold out. He gave our people to those hijackers." She turned to face the Darksiders who were crowding around. "Rolf sold us out," she repeated. "Betrayed us to ruthless people for money."

Cade stood up. "We're only guessing at the moment," he advised her.

"Guessing? What's there to guess?" a man yelled. "You check that credit chip. That would have been Rolf's ticket out of the tunnels. Made on our backs."

Cade felt inclined to agree with him. The way things were stacking up, he and Janek had stumbled on to some well-organized hijacking operation. Only this time, instead of high-tech goods or computers, the merchandise was human. The hijackers were rounding up Darksiders.

The question was why?

What were they doing with the tunnel dwellers?

"You mentioned the reporter who came down here," Cade said. "Kate Bannion?"

Lisa nodded. "I met her up top when I was buying supplies from a friendly store owner. We talked, and she told me who she was. I asked for her help. I was worried about Harry and all our Darksider friends. I didn't know where to turn. So we arranged for her to come down here and do some investigating."

"And she did?"

"Yes. I met her as we'd arranged. She spent a day with us."

Lisa's face clouded over, memories darkening her thoughts.

"What happened?" Cade asked, suspecting the worst.

"There was another raid. The hijackers were scouring the tunnels. I tried to lead her to safety, but we got separated. By the time I managed to search for her, it was too late. She'd disappeared."

"Any idea what happened to her?" Cade asked, sensing Janek listening closely.

"I guess the hijackers took her. Finding out about Rolf makes me think he probably told the hijackers about her being with us."

Janek watched his partner's face as he digested the words. The cyborg didn't need to ask Cade how he was feeling. There was only one answer to that. It was not a reply Janek favored.

He knew his partner only too well, and he knew the way Cade would view Lisa's revelation.

Their present assignment had already plunged them into a tangle of deceit and violence. The fact that Kate Bannion was missing, obviously involved with the hijackers, brought a new perspective to the case.

What had been a tough case now became very personal. And when Cade took things personally, it became unsafe to walk the streets.

8

It was like coming out of a deep, dreamless sleep. Awareness returned with hazy slowness, accompanied by a soothing warmth that seemed to beckon her back into the shroud of security and closeness. Yet into that cocoon of womblike drowsiness intruded light and a growing sense of the tangible world. It pierced the soft darkness, letting in chinks of light, forcing her to open her eyes and accept that sleep was over.

Kate Bannion focused on the gray ceiling above her head, trying to get some kind of grip on reality. Questions began to crowd her sharpening mind, and with the passing seconds the mood of sedated softness vanished, leaving her more alert, curious and angry.

She realized that her sleeplike state had not been natural. Some substance had been administered to her, making her lose consciousness.

But for how long, and where was she now?

Kate wanted answers, a great many answers, to questions that took her all the way back to New York and the Darksiders and her message to Thomas Cade: *I'll make it up to you later. Promise.*

KATE HAD BROKEN the connection and replaced the handset on the vid-phone. She leaned back in the couch, staring at the blank screen for a few seconds. Looking beyond the vid-phone, she took in the misty view of the city through the window of her apartment. It was only eight-thirty in the morning, yet already the day had settled into its mode. Gray and overcast, with soiled clouds sliding through the heavy sky. Rain dribbled down the glass of the large window.

Kate reached for the pot and poured herself a final cup of coffee. She relished the rich aroma and the strong taste. There was no way she would ever compromise and buy the processed stuff. It cost her extra, but she only drank the genuine article. She picked up the coffee beans from a little Cuban delicatessen near her apartment. It was owned by a shriveled old man who claimed he'd been in the second Bay of Pigs invasion force, the one that actually got ashore and retook the island from the stubborn remnants of the Communist regime. That had been more than thirty years ago, so the little Cuban looked the right age, even if his story was ragged around the edges.

She pulled her thoughts back to her current assignment. She had a story of her own to follow. It was going to take her into the lowest levels of New York society, the place where no one from the topside ever went.

Kate was going to talk to the Darksiders.

The Darksiders were the unseen, unacceptable face of the city. The outcasts of a society that pretended they didn't even exist because that was the easiest way to deal with them. No one ever paid any attention to the Darksiders as long as they stayed in their dark, endless tunnels beneath the city.

The Darksiders obliged. They were content. The city and its problems were something alien to them. All they needed and wanted was to be left to their own ways. They were almost a race apart, yet still a section of humanity.

The Darksiders' origins went far back in the city's history. They had always been there, it seemed. Some among them had become homeless due to a run of bad luck, and others didn't fit in, either because of personality flaws or because they had come to despise the normal life of the city and became subterranean dwellers. They evolved over the long years into an organized subculture, with their own strict laws and rules of conduct. There was little unrest among the Darksiders themselves. Prompted by need, they banded together and developed a code of existence that was based on caring for one another and avoiding confrontation with the authorities.

There had been some problems with a certain wild element, yet the Darksiders took care of that themselves. The troublemakers vanished deep in the labyrinth of passages and tunnels that went deep below the city and were never heard from again.

No one knew just how many Darksiders there were. Some said thousands. Others put the figure into the hundreds of thousands. There was no way of coming up with an accurate count because no one ever took the time to make one.

Kate Bannion had been as guilty as anyone when it came to thinking about the Darksiders. She occasionally allowed herself to dwell on their existence when she picked up some small item about them in the news. Apart from that, they remained a shadowy subject just out of her reach.

That is, until she met one of them.

It had been in the Cuban delicatessen. Kate had gone in to pick up some of her coffee. The store had been deserted, except for a thin, pale-faced young girl haggling with the store owner. She wanted to buy canned fruit and was doing her best to knock down the price. In order to get rid of her, the Cuban gave her the cans for a cut price. The girl handed him some crumpled bills, then turned to leave, almost bumping into Kate.

There was something in the young girl's haunted face that touched Kate's heart. She judged herself to be a caring person, and the moment she looked into the dark-ringed eyes set deep in the pale white face, she knew the girl had a great weight hanging over her.

Not a word passed between the two women, and moments later they separated. The girl slipped out of the store.

Kate remained where she was for a few seconds longer, then turned and followed the young girl out of the store. She caught sight of her disappearing down the alley beside the store. Kate followed.

The alley was shadowed, littered with empty packing cases and trash. There was even the burned-out hulk of an old car. Kate walked along the alley, aware of the chilly silence that surrounded her. Stepping into the alley had removed her from the normal sights and sounds of the street and transported her into a world of half light.

For a moment Kate thought she had missed the girl. She peered into the shadows, unsure of herself.

"Why have you followed me?"

The voice came from the darkness where the abandoned car pressed close to the alley wall.

Kate turned and spotted the young girl's slim form. "You looked like someone who needed help."

"From a Topsider?"

Kate frowned. "A Topsider? I don't understand."

"Our word for you. Just like you call us Darksiders."

"You come from the tunnels?"

"Yes."

"I didn't realize you came out to buy your food."

"We don't all steal."

Kate smiled nervously. "That's not what I meant."

The girl edged out from the shadows.

"One of the children needed fruit. She's been ill."

"Something is troubling you, and I can tell it's more serious than just an ill child. Are you in some kind of trouble? Maybe I can help."

"How can you help?"

"I work for one of the city's newspapers. By writing about your problem, I can call attention to it, perhaps bring about changes for the better."

The girl laughed. The sound had a bitter edge to it.

"Topsiders helping us?"

"We don't all turn our backs," Kate said.

The girl dropped a can of fruit. It rolled across the alley, and Kate bent to pick it up. She held it out, noticing that the hand reaching for it was very white, the flesh almost translucent in its paleness. When the girl's fingers brushed her own, Kate felt foolish the second she acknowledged the girl's flesh was warm. She wondered just what she'd been expecting.

"Could you help?" the girl asked suddenly. Her voice echoed the desperation in her eyes.

"I can try. Tell me what's troubling you."

"They're taking Darksiders. They come at night with their lights and their guns and they take our friends away. If anyone interferes, they are beaten. Sometimes killed."

"Who's doing this?" Kate asked. "And why?"

"No one knows. If you really want to help, come and talk with us."

"I will. Tell me where and when."

"Do you know the old Link Tunnel? The one they closed in '47? You can reach it from the Battery Interchange. There's a service tunnel at the end of Platform-1. Walk along it for a quarter mile and you reach the Link. I can meet you there."

"When?" Kate asked.

"I need time to talk with friends. Convince them you're genuine." She stared at Kate. "Are you?"

"Yes. By the way, I'm Kate. Kate Bannion."

She held out her hand. The girl studied it for long seconds before she took it, gripping Kate's hand tightly.

"Lisa," she said softly. "Kate, I'm scared."

"There's something you haven't told me," Kate said. "It's more than just a lot of people going. Am I right?"

Lisa nodded, tears welling up in her eyes. "Last time they came, they took my man. They took Harry, and I'm certain I'll never see him again."

Kate reached out and took the slim body in her arms, holding Lisa close, and knew she had to do something to help.

MIDMORNING the following day found her in the service tunnel. Clad in a one-piece jumpsuit, her compact tape machine over her shoulder, Kate followed the shadowy figure of the transit cop she had paid to show her into the tunnel. He'd been full of himself, only too eager to help her because he recognized her from a photograph in the newspaper when she'd had a big story printed some months back. That and the roll of dollars she'd slipped him turned his initial surliness into fawning eagerness.

"Now you take care in there," he'd advised, playing the big brother. "It can be dangerous. Those Darksiders are harmless enough when let alone, but they don't always take kindly to strangers. So watch yourself."

He brandished his electro-stick to emphasize his words. The look in his eye made Kate feel he wasn't exactly thinking of her in such a brotherly way.

As they had moved deeper into the tunnel system, Kate felt the closeness edge in on her. The confines of the dim tube, with its dripping water and loose floor, added to her discomfort. She had no love for underground places. The darkness and the odd smells, the echoing sounds that seemed to rattle around forever, all went toward unsettling her. But Kate had been in grim places before, and even if she didn't like them, she squared her shoulders and pushed on. She would do her job, but she was damned if she was going to enjoy it.

Her guide halted, turning, his face grinning at her from the glow of his flashlight. He jerked a thumb over his shoulder.

"Down the ramp. At the end you'll find yourself in the old subway tunnel. After that you're on your own, because nothing could get me to go any farther."

Kate refrained from giving him the answer that was on the tip of her tongue. She simply turned and carried on walking, flicking on her own powerful flashlight. The beam danced ahead of her as she reached the ramp and followed it down to where it merged with the larger, and seemingly darker, main tunnel. Only when she reached this section did she turn to look back. The Link Tunnel was deserted. Her guide had gone.

The heavy gloom of the tunnel closed around her. It felt almost alive. She knew it was simply the effect of the darkness and the close, stale air. Underfoot the flooring was loose and littered with trash. Her feet sank into soft substances she just didn't want to know about. She began to hear soft noises, scratchy, rustling sounds, occasionally accompanied by harsh squeaks. Kate knew what caused those sounds. An involuntary shiver coursed down her spine. The shaft of light from the flash picked up the reflection from beady red eyes. They were watching her movements.

The tunnel seemed to go on forever. The darkness extended both in front of and behind her now. Kate began to feel isolated, alone. She walked for what seemed an eternity.

Where was Lisa?

Had she forgotten their arrangement? Perhaps she had been delayed.

Then a voice came out of the darkness around her, soft, almost a whisper, and Lisa's pale features moved into the pool of light cast by the flash.

"You came," she said, surprise in her voice.

"I told you I would," Kate replied. "Hey, can we get out of this damn tunnel? It gives me the creeps."

"I like the darkness," Lisa said. "It's safe...or it was, until those men started coming and stealing our people."

"That's why I'm here," Kate told her. "To see if we can find out what's going on and where they're taking your friends."

Lisa led the way along the gloomy tunnel. Here she was in her element. She moved with ease, comfortable in the shadows and totally unafraid of the atmosphere. She ignored the scurrying rats.

A quarter of an hour later she was leading Kate through narrow tunnels, some lit by bulbs dangling from wires attached to the ceilings. Power was obtained by tapping into electricity cables. In other sections light was provided by oil lamps or sputtering torches that filled the air with stinging fumes.

Kate began to see signs of habitation as they moved deeper into the honeycomb of interconnecting tunnels. She noticed, too, that as they traveled they were descending. The tunnel complex existed on a number of levels, each successive one deeper than its neighbor. The deeper they got, the more people they came across. Although Kate sensed some reserve, she quickly became aware of the gentleness of the tunnel dwellers. There was no open hostility, simply suspicion because she was a stranger. The moment Lisa explained that Kate was there to try to help find out why their people were being taken, the journalist found herself surrounded by anxious faces, each with a personal story to tell.

They had lost husbands. Sons. Brothers. Only a few women had been taken. Young, healthy women.

Following the declaration of who had been taken came the inevitable fearful questions.

Who were the hijackers working for?

Why had the people been taken?

Where were they?

Kate had sympathized with them, trying desperately to comfort them, and promising that she would do everything in her power to locate their missing friends and relatives.

Even as she followed Lisa from tunnel to tunnel, listening to the people, her active mind was seeking a solution, but she had no ready answers.

From the information she'd been able to glean, it appeared that the numbers of missing already ran into the hundreds.

That many people would present a problem when it came to moving them around. Which meant transport of some kind, something familiar on the road so it wouldn't create too much interest.

A large, covered trailer? Hauled by a diesel tractor? There were dozens of those on the roads each day, moving all kinds of goods around. Who would notice those?

Kate filed the possibility away for further investigation.

Hours had slipped by. Kate had become so absorbed by her dealings with the tunnel people that she forgot time. It was only when Lisa drew her into a small room off some tunnel deep below the city that she realized how weary she was. For the first time since coming belowground she glanced at her watch and saw it was late afternoon.

"Hungry?" Lisa asked.

Kate nodded, too absorbed in inspecting the room to speak.

Lisa's home, small and primitive by normal standards, had a coziness that drew Kate into its embrace. The first thing she noticed was the tidiness. Everything had its own niche. Nothing seemed out of place. Her few belongings were obviously well cared for. They had seen long years of use with other owners before coming into her possession.

As Kate watched, Lisa drew water from a plastic container and poured it into a small pan, which she placed on a single electric ring. While the water boiled, she spooned coffee from a small jar into a pair of thick mugs.

"I hope you like it black and unsweetened," Lisa said.

"Right now," Kate said, "I'm ready for anything. You know something, Lisa, I can't remember the last time I did so much walking."

"Kate," Lisa began, "is there...I mean, can you do anything?"

"I can give it a damn good try," Kate assured her. "I've got a few good contacts. I can have questions asked. And I do know someone who might be able to open a few doors."

She was thinking about Cade. If anyone could pick up a lead to what was happening down here in the tunnels, Cade was the man. Once she had her information together, she would present it to him.

Later Lisa took her on a further tour of the tunnels. Kate found she was becoming fascinated by the culture that existed so strongly beneath the city. What caught her imagination was the trust and genuine concern the Darksiders had for one another. There was little envy or distrust. Families and groups existed together with ease. Lisa explained that there were unwritten but closely observed rules. They were laws that no one would break, because if they did, there would be instant justice served. Everything that was done, said or planned was for the good of the overall community. Self-aggrandizement was frowned upon. Greed and deceit were not tolerated. And within those laws the Darksiders lived in a state of almost complete harmony.

That was her impression until Kate saw another side to the Darksider face, when she met a man called Rolf. He had been introduced to her as one of the community leaders. A man who held a position of influence due to his powerful presence. Rolf was known as an elder, because he had the authority to command others. Kate met him and, for some reason, instantly disliked the man. She recognized him as the universal bully, who knew his strength and used it to intimidate others. Rolf clearly knew this. It showed in his manner and the coldness in his eyes. As an outsider Kate viewed him through unblinkered eyes, and what she saw frightened her. Rolf, she decided, was a dangerous man.

For his part, Rolf made no attempt to hide his contempt for Kate.

"I suppose you've told everyone you're here to help them? To expose the cruel exploitation of the Darksiders?"

"Something like that," Kate replied. "Why? You have a reason to think I'm lying?"

"It's a thought. Face it, Bannion, you work in a business that thrives on other people's troubles. It's what newspapers make their money on. A story like ours could sell quite a few editions.''

"If that's the way your mind works," Kate replied, "then you're in a sorry state."

Rolf studied her, his bitter eyes raking her body. He made no attempt to conceal his inner thoughts. Kate saw it all in his face.

"Why object if someone tries to help?"

"We don't need your help," Rolf said. "We look after our own. Always have."

"Tell that to the ones the hijackers took," Lisa snapped suddenly. "Maybe it'll give them some comfort wherever they are. If they're still alive."

She turned and walked away, her slim shoulders hunched in anger.

"She has a point," Kate said. "You haven't exactly done much to stop this business, have you? How many times have the hijackers hit? Enough to make you want to organize some kind of defence against them? So why haven't you?"

She left the question hanging in midair as she hurried to catch up with Lisa. She felt Rolf's cold eyes on her all the way.

Later that night, huddled inside Lisa's cozy room, Kate shared the girl's meager food and listened to her taped information.

"Can you take me back in the morning?" she asked. "I have gathered information that might help me to make a start in my investigation. But I need to talk to my people about it."

Lisa showed her disappointment, but her common sense told her that Kate had to return to the outside if she was going to do anything with the information she had gathered.

"All right, Kate. I'll miss you, though."

"Hey, it doesn't mean we can't see each other again. I'd like to come back, Lisa, when this is all over. Talk to your people again. Get to know them better."

"Even Rolf?" Lisa asked with a half smile on her pale lips.

Kate shook her head. "No, not Rolf. Lisa, I don't trust him. Can't tell you why, but my instincts are telling me he's no damn good."

"You're not the only one. A number of us have been quietly questioning Rolf's failure to handle the hijackers. There's something odd going on."

They were about to settle down to sleep when the silence was broken by the distant, unmistakable sound of gunfire. Shouts and screams echoed along the tunnels.

"Not again!" Lisa whispered, her eyes wide with terror.

"The hijackers?" Kate asked.

"Yes." Lisa scrambled by Kate, pushing aside the blanket that covered the entrance. "Kate, we have to get out of here. They're very close."

Kate snatched up her recorder, then followed Lisa as she hurried along the tunnel. She didn't ask any questions but simply trusted the Darksider to lead her to safety.

The sound of gunfire came closer. The thump of heavy boots thundered in her ears. Kate ran, breath catching in her throat. Ahead of her, Lisa's slim body twisted easily around the bends in the tunnel they were following. Kate maintained her pace despite the uneven ground.

Suddenly Lisa took another turn, cutting along a narrow side tunnel. The move had taken place so quickly that Kate overshot the spot. She slithered to a stop, tripped and fell to her knees. Muttering under her breath, she clambered to her feet and headed for the side tunnel.

She had no time to reach it.

Armed figures, clad in dark nylon coveralls, filled the tunnel. They wore hoods over their heads, and black visors hid their faces.

Kate turned about, only to find that her way was blocked by more figures. These were Darksiders, and Kate saw that they were also carrying guns.

She recognized the one leading them.

It was Rolf.

"You bastard," Kate yelled. "I knew I was right not to trust you!"

Rolf advanced on her, his autopistol leveled.

"And I guess I was right about you. I said you were trouble."

"You haven't seen anything yet," Kate raged.

Rolf gestured for one of his men to grab her.

Kate let him get close, then swung her recorder by its strap. The solid weight caught him across the side of the head, knocking him against the wall of the tunnel. He stumbled, bleeding from one cheek. Kate saw a second figure moving toward her and she lashed out again. A hand reached out and snatched the recorder from her fingers, and too late Kate remembered the hooded figures behind her. She fought them every step of the way as they tried to subdue her. Despite her struggles they overwhelmed her and dragged her to the ground.

"Not so tough now?" Rolf said with a grin, peering down at her.

He gestured, and one of the hooded men knelt beside Kate. She watched, fascinated as he produced a glittering syringe, slipping off the cap at the end of the needle. Then he brought the syringe to her arm, pushing up the sleeve of her jumpsuit. She wriggled, realizing what was about to happen, but there was nothing she could do. The hands holding her down were too strong. The cold prick of the needle was followed by the hard feel of it entering her arm. Moments later a warm glow began to engulf her body.

"Can't say it's been a pleasure," Rolf said. His voice sounded a million miles away.

Kate stared up at him. His features wavered, began to dissolve before her eyes.

"...an interesting trip..."

Rolf's final words barely penetrated the mist of warmth flowing over her. Kate struggled, but couldn't be sure her body was responding to her commands. She felt herself slipping away from reality. Her awareness decreased and she felt numb, weightless. Sight and sound and feeling had all but gone. She was losing everything. Her entire being was shutting down....

KATE SAT UP on the bunk bed where she'd been lying. She inspected the small room she was in, her eyes picking out the details.

No windows. Illumination by a harsh strip light in the ceiling. The walls and floor were all constructed out of the same dull material. A bland gray color. It looked more like a prison cell...or a cabin. Was she on a ship? Heading where?

She stood up slowly, feeling her legs tremble as she put weight on them. She walked the length of the room, inspecting its construction. The single door was locked. She would have been surprised if it hadn't been. There wasn't even a handle on her side.

Standing in the middle of the floor, she became aware of a gentle vibration. Placing her hand against the wall, she realized she could feel it there. The vibration suggested power. A great deal of power. Again Kate thought of a ship.

The door slid open with a soft hum, startling her. Before Kate could reach it, the opening was blocked by the gleaming form of a chrometal android carrying a tray of food.

"Time for you to eat, Miss Bannion," the android said.

"Where am I?" she asked.

"Cabin 12, deck 3."

"What vessel?"

The android turned to look at her. Its amber eyes surveyed her for a time.

"You are on board the ore freighter *Lexus-6*. We are two days out from Orbit Platform Pegasus-2. Our course is set for the Asteroid Belt, with touchdown on Lexus-9 in twenty-eight days."

The android placed the tray on the bunk, then left the cabin. Kate barely registered the door sliding shut. Her mind whirled as she absorbed the information the robot had given her.

She *was* on a ship, but not an oceangoing vessel. She was on a deep-space freighter on its way to the mining colonies of the Asteroid Belt. Earth already lay two days behind her, and with every passing second she was being taken farther into space, away from everything she knew and away from anyone who cared for her.

For long moments Kate was plunged into deep despair. She gazed wildly around the sparse cabin—which she now considered her prison cell—and realized that for the first time in her life she was truly and utterly alone. There was no one here to help her.

Not even Cade, the one man she could always count on.

Even he was out of reach and probably unaware of her predicament.

She was involved in the biggest story of her career, but the way things were going, there was no way she would be able to write it. Not even for her obituary.

9

"You'll like this, T.J.," Janek said, walking into the main office with a computer readout in his hand. He deposited the sheet on Cade's desk. "Everything is starting to fit in place."

Cade scanned the sheet. The information was laid out neatly, each strand connecting to the next like a family tree.

"I did some in-depth scanning," Janek explained. "Feldstet and Dolan were both receiving impressive payments into their bank accounts way beyond the scope of their salaries. The inputs came via a series of dead drops, but even they have a source. I set up the computer to follow the trail of each irregular payment. Somebody thought they were being clever by paying through a complicated chain of dummy accounts, all by electronic transfer. I don't suppose they ever considered anyone would bother to check through so many transactions. Every payment originated from the office of Hamilton Lasall. Max Lippin's employer."

Cade took a closer look at the computer readout as Janek continued the rundown.

"Rolf?"

"The same, T.J. Lasall was paying Rolf, too, and Jak Regis. There are a number of other names on the list, as well, and I ran a check on them. Quite a mixed bunch. Most of them already known to the law-enforcement agencies."

"The hired help. The guys that do the dirty work. What do the lines under the names mean?"

"They're dead, T.J. They tie in with the people we tangled with on the freeway and the hit men I ran into at Feldstet's apartment building. And Rolf's pair of gunmen."

"This gets wilder by the minute." Cade leaned back in his chair. "What does it all lead to, apart from someone trying to stop us digging too deep? Just what the hell have we stumbled into?"

"Here is an indication," Janek said. "The trucking company in Newark. The one the panel truck is registered to. Guess who is the company lawyer?"

"Lasall? He's a busy guy."

"Before you ask, T.J., I already checked his client list," Janek said. "For the past three years his main source of income has been Lexus Incorporated. One of those multinational companies. Deals in everything you can think of. Deeply into electronic and industrial manufacture. Owned by Randolph Boon. One of those old-time magnates. A tough businessman who figures he's better than the rest. Runs the company like a private kingdom."

"Has Lasall any stake in the company?"

"Owns a sizable chunk of shares apparently," Janek said.

"This keeps on getting better," Cade remarked. "Did you turn up anything on the phone cards?"

"Had the central computer run a check. They came up with the number of the freight company in Newark. The other one is proving hard to break. It's one of those illegal circuit-runner cards. They'll get to the number eventually."

Circuit-runner cards were used by individuals who didn't want their number exposed. It meant that a party could receive calls, via a complicated set of illegal dead-drop numbers that rerouted the call back and forth before connecting with the destination. Circuit-runner calls were nonvisual, and the individual on the receiving end of the call remained unknown, his voice being electronically altered.

Cade banged his fist down on the desk and swore between gritted teeth.

"And Kate's right in the middle of all this shit."

"We've two leads," Janek pointed out. "The freight company and Hamilton Lasall. Perhaps it's time to make some house calls."

"Right on, pal," Cade said. "I'll handle Lasall first. Even if I don't get anything from him, at least I can make him believe we're getting close. It could scare him into making a move."

Janek sighed. "That means you want me to stay out of it. You're going to start bending the rules again, Thomas."

Cade gave a tight grin. "I don't want you breathing over my shoulder like my conscience, partner. If you don't see it, you can't gripe about it."

"So what do you want me to do?"

"Go talk to your computers. Pull anything that might tie in with the info we have. I don't give a damn how vague it is. Just do a search, then list all the probables and possibles. What I'd really like is something on Connor. That guy is involved—I know it."

"He's covered his tracks well if he's involved," Janek said.

"Like Milt said, Connor's a sly one. He's been around too long to leave anything easily traceable. You'll have to turn over some big stones to find where his stash is. Hell, partner, I don't need to tell you what to do."

"Exactly," Janek muttered frostily, and headed for his computer room.

CADE FLOORED the gas pedal, sending the cruiser rocketing along the street. It bounced over the potholes, sending silver sprays of rainwater across the crowded sidewalks. The rain had stopped, but the day was still gray and cloudy. The sky hung low over the city, threatening, and the ever-present pollution cast a pall across the horizon.

New York had managed to retain much of its original flavor at street level, despite the ecological and social changes that had occurred during the first half of the century. The rich got richer and the poor just managed to survive. The division between the groups had become noticeably greater. As the city declined at street level, the designers and builders created physical barriers. These were in the shape of elevated roads and walkways that formed links between the towering buildings of the city. When new structures were built, the high-level road and walkway systems were increased, until New York became a two-tier city. The ultrarich, who inhabited the upper reaches, never descended to street level. They worked and played in their protected environment. This section of the city became known as the Heights. In between the two extremes were the offices of the executive class.

Hamilton Lasall had his office in the Wall Street section. The area remained the hub of the country, dictating the rise and fall of the financial heartbeat. Cade parked the cruiser outside one of the elevator banks, flashing his badge at the KC patrolman who had approached him the moment he got out of the vehicle.

"Keep an eye on it for me," Cade growled, and the android touched a gloved hand to the peak of his cap.

Inside the elevator bank Cade located the car that would take him to the level where Lasall's offices were located. He stepped inside, using his Justice Department card to override the security lock.

"Which level do you require?" asked the soothing tones of the car's computer.

"Twenty-third," Cade said.

The car rose smoothly, its speed increasing as it soared up through the levels. It slowed and stopped with a gentle sigh, the doors opening to deposit Cade on floor twenty-three.

It was all glass and polished steel, hidden lights casting a soft glow over the thick pile carpet. Gentle background music filtered out from concealed speakers. Panoramic Plexiglas windows allowed a breathtaking view across the city when the mist cleared, but at this height the buildings and walkways were frequently wreathed in soft mist. Huge vid-screens showed ever-changing financial information interspersed with commercials for exotic vacations to idyllic locations around the world and beyond.

Cade made his way along the walk, checking out the office frontages until he found Lasall's.

The wide smoked-glass doors swished open, and a shapely android receptionist beamed up at Cade as he approached her desk.

"May I help you?"

Cade showed her his badge.

"Tell Hamilton Lasall I want to see him."

"I'll see if Mr. Lasall is free," the receptionist said, still smiling as she reached for the phone.

Cade shook his head. "He doesn't have a choice," he said, and briskly headed toward the big doors that bore Lasall's name.

"But you can't..." the receptionist called, her voice incredulous.

Cade shoved the doors open and strode into the spacious office. It seemed to go on forever, a wide, expansive room with a low ceiling and a sweeping picture window behind the vast desk. To the far right, three steps allowed access to a sunken lounge area complete with leather seats and a large-screen TV. The walls were hung with well-framed paintings, and a number of modern sculptures stood on neat plinths.

The slim, dark-haired man behind the desk watched Cade's entrance with hooded eyes. He wore a close-fitting gray suit and a simple-looking roll-neck sweater that had probably cost a small fortune. As Cade came across the room, the man pushed back his high-backed executive chair and rose to his feet. He raised a slender hand, snapping his fingers.

Cade caught movement off to his left. He turned in that direction and saw the lunging bulk of the bodyguard. Taller than Cade and wider, the guard led his rush with his close-cropped bullet head, and his hands spread with anticipation. There was no evidence of any expression on his face as he closed in on Cade.

The man was massive in build and powerful, but he lacked finesse and agility. Cade easily sidestepped the initial lunge, then turned and drove a clenched fist into his side. The blow was hard and uncompromising, and the bodyguard winced at the pain from cracked ribs. He turned, sweeping a huge fist in a backhand blow that would have delivered serious harm to Cade's head had it landed. He was able to duck beneath it, hammering his right elbow into the man's lower back. The bodyguard grunted and fell to his knees. Cade moved up behind him, hands at the back of his skull, then shoved down hard, driving the head against the solid desk top. The bodyguard slipped from Cade's hands to the floor.

Cade straightened up and eased his badge out of his pocket. He turned toward the dark-haired man and flashed the badge at him.

"Sit down, Lasall."

Hamilton Lasall's eyes registered the name on the badge, and recognition flickered across his face. Then a blank look settled on his face, and he moved to sit back in the swivel chair, all the time watching Cade closely.

"Feel a little out of your league, Cade?"

"In your case, Lasall, I'm on familiar ground."

The lawyer's mouth tightened. "Are you implying that I'm guilty of something?"

"Let's say I'm getting there. A few more loose ends, Lasall, then I'll be back with the 'cuffs and you'll be on your way to the Asteroid Belt."

Lasall made light of Cade's remark. He actually smiled, but it never reached his eyes. For a moment his eyes flicked back and forth across the room, then settled back on Cade.

"What exactly are you accusing me of?"

"We both know what you've been up to, Lasall. And you might have got away with it if I hadn't picked up a lowlife called Bernie Stenner. You know the type—he had a loose mouth and wanted to talk a deal. Trouble is, I lost him before he managed to give me the full story. But I'm picking it up piece by piece, and it's all falling into place. And you know what? I keep coming across the same name. Guess who it belongs to."

Cade looked mockingly at Lasall, then stepped around the groaning bodyguard and headed for the door.

"You figured it out yet?" he called back over his shoulder. He turned, a finger jabbing at the lawyer. "Yours,

Lasall. Your name. So don't skip town, because I'll be back."

He closed the door and left the suite of offices. He took the elevator back to street level and the waiting cruiser. Inside he picked up the phone and called the office.

"Hi, partner," he said as Janek came on. "I'm on my way back to pick you up. Time we took a swing over to Newark and had a look at that freight company."

"I'll be waiting," Janek said. "How did it go with Lasall?"

Cade smiled. "He'll be on the phone by now, calling his contacts and splitting hairs."

"It could turn out to be too much for the two of us," Janek warned. "If his people feel we're getting too close, they could throw anything at us."

"You don't say?" Cade replied.

Janek sighed. "You just love it when things get hairy."

"I need a little excitement once in a while. Comes from working with an old woman like you."

"Hah!" Janek said, and put the phone down.

Cade swung away from the curb, forcing his way into the traffic and ignoring the yells he received. He pushed the cruiser along at a steady clip.

His mind was working overtime, trying to make sense out of the jumble of facts and figures Janek had thrown at him. The cybo could set the mess out neat and tidy in his computer brain, retaining any amount of information, while Cade had to use old-fashioned human logic. Without all the trimmings, Cade at least knew he was looking at one hell of a conspiracy. One that involved the law, high-priced lawyers and now some multinational company. The only thing missing was the motivation for it, the payoff, the single fact that would make perfect sense out of the tangled web.

He had swung through the intersection onto Fulton, heading back toward Broadway, when he became aware of a sleek black limousine running parallel with his cruiser. The vehicle had dark-tinted windows, and there was something odd about the way it ran even with the cruiser. Cade was about to make an evasive move when he spotted a second limousine, also black, on the opposite side. A small voice inside his head told him to check the rearview mirror, and Cade saw a third car on his tail.

They had him boxed in.

Cade figured he only had seconds before something drastic happened. The elaborate convoy wasn't there to escort him home. He glanced ahead. There was a compact in front, with a fair gap between it and the next vehicle. Cade kept his eye on the compact, and also the side streets. Whatever he did would have to be fast, because he wouldn't get a second try.

He saw a narrow alley coming up. It was only wide enough to take one car at a time. Cade jammed his foot hard down on the gas pedal, feeling the powerful, supercharged cruiser leap forward. He yanked hard on the wheel, rolling as the cruiser slewed to the left, cutting across the front of the limo on that side. He clipped the rear corner of the compact, sending it surging forward, clearing the way for him. The cruiser's engine howled. Tires burned against the pavement as the cruiser shot toward the alley. Cade felt the nose of the limousine clout him midsection, and the cruiser slid off course. He dragged the heavy wheel back, pulling the lurching car on line as it shot for the mouth of the alley.

Behind him the rattle of gunfire rose above the roaring engine. The cruiser's rear window blew out as a stream of slugs shattered the glass. Cade almost lost control as the car lurched wildly into the alley. Sparks trailed behind the cruiser as the body scraped the brickwork on either side, the vehicle bouncing back and forth between the opposing buildings.

Cade caught a glimpse of one limousine following him into the alley. It's windows were powered down to allow armed figures to lean out and open up with autoweapons. Slugs hammered the cruiser's body, and Cade knew it was only a matter of seconds before they found his fuel tank. He felt the cruiser lurch as one rear tire blew. Moments later the other one went, and the cruiser rolled along on steel rims.

Cade snatched up the SPAS, released his door latch and slammed on the footbrake. He exited the slithering cruiser, bracing his back against the wall, and swung the SPAS into position. Cade triggered the autoloader without pause, delivering its seven shots with devastating results. The limousine's windshield disintegrated under the barrage of hot lead, and the occupants were shredded by the close-quarters blasts.

The moment he'd fired the last shot, Cade turned and ran. Behind him the out-of-control limo hit the rear of the stalled cruiser. There was a screech of tortured metal, followed by a solid thump of sound. Cade felt a surge of heat wash over him, and an invisible hand pushed him against the alley wall. The air around him was suddenly full of debris. Turning, he saw the ball of gasoline flame sweep up between the sides of the building, quickly followed by a thick cloud of oily smoke.

Cade pulled his Magnum, peering through the smoke. The approach to the alley was blocked by another black limousine. It remained in place for a few moments longer, then reversed and pulled away.

Cautiously moving along toward the far end of the alley, his gun at the ready, Cade kept a watch for further developments. Nothing happened. The surviving limousines had vanished in the traffic.

Emerging from the alley at the far end, Cade spotted a street cruiser and waved it down. In moments he was on the phone to Janek, telling his partner to book out another car so he could come down to pick Cade up.

"THIS IS BECOMING embarrassing, T.J.," Janek said. He stood by the replacement cruiser, grumbling about the fact that he had been forced to requisition the new car from the car pool.

"Well, thanks for your concern. I'm fine. No scratches. I just nearly got blown away, and all you can do is give me a hard time about a damn car."

"You're not the one who had to go crawling to that droid who runs the car pool. He practically wanted my life history before he'd give me a car."

"Janek—tough titty," Cade said, and climbed behind the wheel of the cruiser. He leaned out the window and waved to the uniformed policeman supervising the alley cleanup. "Talk to you later, Phil."

"Take it easy, T.J.," the officer called with a wave of the hand.

Janek slid into the passenger seat, pulling the door shut. Cade hit the gas pedal and pulled sharply away from the curb, bulling his way into the late-afternoon traffic. Janek was jerked against the back of the seat.

"Take it easy, T.J., or are you deliberately trying to loosen my memory chips?"

"Quit griping." Cade eased off the pedal, glancing at his partner. "You get any more from your PC buddies?"

Janek ignored the jibe.

"I did what you suggested and searched all sources for tie-in data. The most significant thing I came across was the death of a geologist named Frakin. He died about seven months back. Killed in a mugging, the report says."

"So?"

"I also picked up the information that Lexus has a sub-division I missed first time around. A mining operation. On Lexus-9, one of the asteroids. You with me so far, T.J.?"

Cade nodded. "Don't be so melodramatic, Janek. If you've got something, for Christ's sake spit it out."

He swerved wildly, narrowly missing the rear end of a New York transit bus. Racing along the side of the bus, Cade gave an admonishing blast with his siren.

Janek sat back, patiently waiting for his partner to work off his frustrations.

"These shameless bus drivers think they own the road," Cade muttered, yanking the cruiser back into its lane.

"He obviously doesn't realize the system belongs to you personally," Janek murmured flippantly.

"What? Oh, funny guy."

"Can I continue?"

Cade waved his hand. He had found a half-smoked cigar in his pocket and was in the process of lighting it. "We got as far as Lexus-9. Real dump of a place."

"You know it?"

"Did a spell there when I was with the Marine Space Corps. Got transferred to them after the war in '36. Spent four damn years in the colonies. Real pain. Back then the mining operations were running wild. Lexus-9 had a mean reputation. Funny, I didn't connect when you mentioned Lexus earlier."

"Could be you're getting old, T.J.," Janek said dryly.

Cade expelled thick clouds of smoke. "What's the death of this geologist got to do with Lexus-9?"

"About a month before he died, Frakin had completed a survey for Lexus-9. That much is on the records. I'm still trying to find the actual report. There should be a copy kept on file. I haven't been able to unearth it yet, and that makes me suspicious."

"You and me both," Cade said.

They were still deliberating the facts when Cade hit the Holland Tunnel. They emerged on the far side, Cade easing the cruiser along the on ramp for the Newark Link Expressway.

Janek picked up the phone, tapping in a number that would link him with the computer back at their office. He used the sensors built into the tips of his fingers to connect himself to the modem-pad in the handset. Leaning back in his seat, Janek began to absorb the information coming across the line. The transfer was completed in less than a minute, and he put the phone down with a satisfied smile on his lips.

"You can't beat a good information surge," he said. "Really sets me up."

"Yeah? Well, apart from giving you a high, does it tell us anything useful?"

"Central computer managed to locate the original report Frakin entered. Somebody tried losing it by shifting it to Pittsburgh South Information Center. They had it logged under Miscellaneous. If there were any queries, all they had to say was that it must have been mistakenly rerouted."

"Why not just erase it?"

"Can't be done, T.J.," Janek explained. "Frakin's report had to be submitted to the local information pool. He'd do that as a matter of course. Federal law. There's no way information in that system can be erased. But a smart hacker could get it moved. Lost somewhere in the network.''

''So what does it tell us?''

''Apparently Lexus-9 had opened an extremely rich new seam of pure titanium. It was way down below any of their previous levels. Frakin's investigation showed the area to be unfit for working. He found a band of unstable strata covering the extent of the seam. It could break up any time once mine operations began and cause massive cave-ins.''

''Lexus wouldn't take that information too well,'' Cade said. ''Titanium's at a premium just now. Hell of a lot of money to be made from it. Military contracts. Robotics.''

Suddenly Janek sat bolt upright. He snapped his fingers, a triumphant ''yes'' coming from his lips.

''What, already?'' Cade snapped, realizing that his partner had figured something out.

''You have to give it to them,'' Janek said, admiration in his tone. ''It's clever. Even inspired.''

''What, for Christ's sake?''

''Why the Darksiders are being hijacked, T.J. The reason they're being taken.''

''I'm getting there,'' Cade lied.

''Hah,'' Janek said. ''You haven't figured it out yet, have you?'' A slight smile curled the edge of his mouth.

''All right,'' Cade snapped back. ''So I haven't figured it out, mega-brain. You want to tell me or play smart-ass all day?''

Janek twisted around in his seat to face him.

''They're using the Darksiders for two reasons. First because they are expendable members of society. No one really pays any attention to them during the normal run of things. Who is going to miss them? Only other Darksiders, and they won't say anything because they don't trust the authorities and also they want to be left alone. Are we in agreement so far?''

Cade nodded.

"The second and most important reason," Janek explained, "is based on the fact that Darksiders are ideal workers for the ore mines. They exist in a subterranean environment. Which means they're used to living in the near dark. Their eyes and their metabolism have adjusted to it. Darksiders are at home down below the surface. Bring them into the light, and they beg to be let underground again."

"Janek, you son of a bitch," Cade said. "You hit the jackpot. Lexus is using the Darksiders as illegal workers in the unsafe mine. They lost Frakin's report and brought in the Darksiders because they daren't use regular miners. The Darksiders can't complain because they don't have anyone to back them. And as far as the authorities are concerned, Lexus has never opened the new seam."

"The Darksiders are losers all the way down the line, T.J. People are hardly aware of their existence, and even if their plight were known, who would bother to fight for their rights? A few hundred less means a reduction in the Darksider problem. And the mine company gets free labor fit for the task. With plenty of replacements for the ones who die."

"An operation on this scale would bring in big bucks," Cade said. "Lexus is getting the titanium out free. The payoffs will be small change for whoever is running it. Hell, no damn wonder we have so many guns out to blow us away."

"It must have upset someone really badly when we stumbled on the operation," Janek observed. "And all because Bernie Stenner tried to make a deal with you."

"Okay, partner," Cade said. "Let's not waste what Bernie started for us. I think it's time we got the ball rolling."

"Two other items of news," Janek said. "The limo you totalled was registered to the freight company. The guy who runs the company is one Leo Krask."

"Fat Leo?" Cade said.

"That's one of his aliases," Janek answered. "You know him?"

Cade nodded. "Seen him in lineups a number of times. Never been involved face-to-face, but his name has figured in certain cases over the years. He's always been in the rackets."

"It appears he still is," Janek said.

Cade peered ahead into the stream of traffic, then stomped on the accelerator.

"Let's go say hello to the fat man."

10

The light was fading fast by the time Cade pulled the cruiser to a stop near the freight yard. To the south lay the seemingly endless sprawl of Newark's combined air and shuttle port. From the blast-scorched launch pads the passenger and cargo shuttles lifted off for the orbiting space platform complex.

With the mounting evidence they were gathering, Cade and Janek found the close proximity of the shuttle port taking on a new significance.

The hijacked Darksiders, shipped to the freight yard, could be quickly moved to the port and into cargo bays of waiting shuttles.

Cade stared across the lowering sky to the shimmering halo of light hanging over the shuttle port complex and found himself wondering if Kate Bannion had become a member of one of those illegal cargos. Was she up there somewhere? Maybe already on her way to the distant Asteroid Belt?

"We'll find out where she is, T.J.," Janek spoke up beside him.

Cade glanced at him. "Damn right we will," he said.

Pulling out his autopistol, Cade checked that it was fully loaded.

"You expecting to use that?" Janek asked as he exited the cruiser.

"Depends on the answers I get," his partner replied.

"Is that the best way to approach this problem, T.J.?" Janek asked.

"It's the only way, partner. Besides, I haven't been greeted with open arms when I've asked questions before. Now rack up that SPAS, pass it over and cut the chattiness."

Janek accepted temporary defeat. He knew there was no reasoning with Cade when he was like this. The human condition tended to change rapidly, giving no indication of how it was going to alter. Calmness and sanity could be replaced instantly by reckless anger, and judgment became immediately clouded by those unstable emotions that seemed to dominate human behavior to an alarming extent. Janek sighed wearily. It was, he knew, one of the penalties for having a human for a partner. The cold, clear logic that controlled his judgment had no chance within the human animal. They were still savages under the skin, ruled by petty, almost base, reactions to each and every situation they faced. The human race had established itself as the most advanced form of biological life on earth. People were, by cyborg standards, less than advanced—despite the fact that they had created and built the robots.

It was a paradox. The creators had become less than the beings they had created. The cyborgs had been fashioned in man's image, given his view of the world, then set free to exist alongside their creator. Somewhere in the process the cyborgs had gained an advantage over man. Perhaps it was due to their electronic intelligence—the manufactured brain that functioned on pure logic, not illogical thought processes. The oddity was that man, for all his faults, was still capable of greatness. There were the classic artists. The musicians and writers. Intellectual geniuses. So much that had to be accepted as good in the human world.

Yet just a step behind was the base side of man. Janek saw this in his work alongside Cade. The horror and violence. The suffering that the human animal visited upon his own species. Evil stood side by side with good, and there seemed no depths to which the animal side of man could not plummet. It was a complex state of affairs, enough to reduce logical thought to a mockery. But it was the way things were. Janek understood that, and also knew there was nothing he could do to alter it. No more than his human partner Cade could in the short term.

Janek wandered along the street, studying the high fence around the freight yard.

"I can't detect anything out of the ordinary," he said on his return. "How do we do this, T.J.?"

"Janek, tell me, how many times have we done this kind of thing before?"

"Exact figure, or do you want a yearly average?"

Cade threw his arms wide in a gesture of defeat and walked away. After a moment Janek followed, muttering in a low monotone.

Arc lights on tall poles illuminated the freight yard. The high fence was topped by electro-beams capable of frying a man in seconds. The gates were secured by internally controlled ram bolts.

"Here's one to tax your circuits," Cade said as they paused at the gates.

Janek studied the layout for a few seconds. He nodded to himself, then moved to the gates. He gripped the thick steel mesh and tore a hole so he could reach through. Cade watched as the cyborg gripped one of the ram bolts, his powerful fingers closing with crushing power against the chrome-steel shafts. Janek set himself, then began to lift. The ram bolt held for a few seconds, then began to withdraw from its locking tube. Cade wasn't sure of the exact pressure that held the ram bolts secure, but he understood the principles behind the pneumatic power packs that held them in the closed position. Janek's steady lift had the desired effect. The bolt slid free. There was a hiss of air from the main pneumatic power pack. A seal split, and the bolt suddenly offered no more resistance. Janek shoved the gate open and stepped into the freight compound.

"Let's go, T.J.," Janek said in a fair imitation of his partner. "Time to kick some ass."

They crossed the compound. There were rows of semi-trailers parked along the eastern edge of the compound. Way across the far side of the area the service bays showed some activity as the night crews carried out maintenance checks on vehicles.

Cade led the way to the office block, the combat shotgun ready in his hands. The lower floor was in darkness. Leo Krask had his living quarters on the top floor where Cade spotted light behind the windows.

There were two armed guards at the entrance to the building.

"No time for fancy games," Cade said.

He slid into the shadows alongside the building and eased in the direction of the entrance. Janek followed close on his heels. They got within range of the gunmen without difficulty. The pair were busy talking and weren't paying any attention to their surroundings.

Cade straightened up and stepped in close behind one man, touching him on the shoulder. The surprised guard turned, his mouth opening to speak. Cade whacked the barrel of the SPAS alongside his jaw. The guy spun around, dropping his subgun. He followed it to the ground seconds later as Cade hit him a second time.

Janek had disarmed the second guard and already had him pinned against the wall, feet off the ground. The cyborg watched Cade cuff his man.

"Ask him nicely to unlock the door," Cade said.

"Did you hear that?" Janek asked, increasing the pressure of his fingers around the guard's throat until the man frantically nodded. Janek lowered him to the ground, pushing him to the digital lock that secured the entrance door.

"Do it right the first time," Janek suggested, "because you won't get a second chance."

The guard punched in the sequence code. The doors clicked and swung open. Janek marched his captive in, and Cade followed, dragging his man along, then dumping him behind the empty reception desk.

"One more favor," Cade said to the gunman. "Get us into the elevator to Krask's apartment."

The man repeated his trick with the elevator code. The car slid to the ground floor, doors opening smoothly. Cade stepped in. Janek followed, with his prisoner. The man didn't need to be instructed this time. He keyed in the floor code, and the elevator rose.

The corridor that led to Krask's apartment was empty. Cade peered out of the elevator, checking it thoroughly. He glanced at the gunman.

"Is Krask on his own?"

The man shook his head. "Three bodyguards. Krask has a couple of visitors in tonight."

"Who?"

"The legal eagles. Lasall and Lippin."

Cade smiled when he heard the names. "There still is a Santa Claus," he said.

"What?" Janek asked.

"How did Lasall get here so fast?" Cade asked.

"Well, I don't know what you mean, but he came in by a hired chopper. Looked like a last-minute visit. He isn't a happy man."

Cade took out a pair of plasti-cuffs. He spun the guard around and secured his hands behind him.

"Hey, I ain't about to warn 'em."

"Hell, I know that, pal," Cade replied, and hit him with the SPAS. The guy crumpled in the corner of the elevator.

Cade calmly started walking along the corridor toward the apartment door.

"I want the key men alive and able to talk," he said to Janek. "The triggers take their chance."

"And we know what that will be," Janek said.

Cade rapped loudly on the door.

"Come on, you guys, we got trouble downstairs," he yelled.

"Do you think such a simple ploy will . . ."

The door rattled, then swung open. The man framed in the opening was large, broad shouldered and carried a squat subgun. He eyed Cade for a few seconds too long before realization set in.

Cade slugged him with the SPAS, driving the weapon up under the guy's heavy jaw. The sound of the blow filled the corridor. The trigger's head snapped back, and blood coursed down his shirtfront. Cade whacked him again, hard in the abdomen. The man doubled over, gasping. Pushing him aside, Cade stepped inside.

Right behind him, Janek stepped in swiftly to disarm the dazed trigger and cuff him.

A second trigger came into view, his weapon raised. He took one look at Cade and Janek and yelled a warning. His weapon arced round, spitting fire. Bullets punctured the wall over Cade's head. He dropped to one knee, leveling the SPAS, and let go with a single shot. The blast caught the trigger in the chest and threw him back into the living room, where he collided with a low table, scattering magazines and drinking glasses before he fell to the floor.

Janek had ducked low and gone for the living room. He headed toward the three carpeted steps, but he was confronted by the surviving trigger. The gunman threw up his handgun, a large, stainless-steel autopistol, and triggered a 3-round burst. Janek took a dive to the floor, then rolled, already firing as he rolled. The hollowpoint slugs impacted against the trigger's lower chest, spiraling up in a devastating path of destruction. The trigger, already dying, staggered back to crash against the wall.

Cade came down the steps at a dead run, almost colliding with Krask, Lasall and Lippin as they hastened in the direction of the front door.

"What the hell are you playing at, Cade?" Max Lippin shouted. "I'll have your badge for this!"

Leo Krask turned to face Cade. His beefy face was flushed and angry. "This is Cade, the SOB you been lettin' walk all over you?" Krask shoved a hand inside his jacket. "I'll show you how to handle him."

Cade didn't say a word. His sweep into the room had brought him directly into Krask's path, and as he reached the man, Cade threw a long, looping right that impacted against Krask's slack jawline with a crack. Krask fell back across a lounger, hitting the floor on his back. He lay staring up at Cade, blood welling from a split lip. When he tried to sit up, Cade bounced the SPAS's barrel off the top of his skull, then reached down and hauled the man's pistol out and shoved it behind his own belt.

"On your feet, Krask," Cade ordered. "It's conversation time."

Krask levered himself upright. He dropped into an armchair, sleeving blood from his mouth. His expression was ugly as he stared up at Cade.

"I have nothin' to say to you."

"Don't be coy, Krask. We've got it all now. Lexus Mining. The Darksiders. You providing the muscle, Lasall the payoffs and legal backup."

"If you know everything, what do you want from me? Go suck, cop," Krask jeered. "You don't have a thing you can take to court. You don't know who you're mixing with."

Cade turned on him. "That's where you're wrong. I'm going to hang you all out to dry, even if it means going to Lexus-9."

"I suppose I better call this in," Janek said, coming over to join Cade.

"Get through to Milt Schuberg. We need some local cops to take these boys in. Have them shipped out to a secure facility. Only our people to know about it. No contact with anyone outside for these three."

"I understand, T.J."

"Can he do this?" Krask demanded.

Cade looked across at Lasall. The lawyer was ashen faced. He knew when he was beaten.

"He can do it, Leo."

"Listen to the man, Leo," Janek suggested. "He's a lawyer. He knows what he's talking about."

Cade said, "Krask, I need straight answers to a couple more questions. Don't screw these up because they're important to you, and damn personal to me. They concern a very good friend of mine. Give me the wrong answers, and you're a dead man. I guarantee that."

Krask's face glistened with sweat as he stared at Cade.

"Kate Bannion. Where is she? And how is she?"

Krask closed his eyes for a few seconds. His heavy jowls shook as he calmed himself.

"She got caught in a Darksider sweep. The snatch team took her along with the rest."

Cade's gut began to churn. He was anticipating Krask's next words.

"We figured she needed silencing. So she was loaded on a freighter with a shipment of Darksiders." Krask stared at Cade, his eyes registering the fear that was making him shake. He didn't want to speak the next words, because he knew they would damn him in the cop's eyes, but he also realized that to deny knowledge would place him in even greater danger.

"She's gone," he said. "I guess by now she'll be on her way to Lexus-9. But I swear I don't know if she's alive or dead."

"Krask, you'd better pray she's alive. Because if I get there too late, I'll be coming for you when I get back. Don't figure being behind bars will save you. Because it won't."

WITHIN THE HOUR the freight yard had been secured. A squad from the Newark Police Department gathered the suspects Cade singled out and bundled them into a department wagon. Under guard the prisoners would be driven to an undisclosed facility and held until Cade decided what steps to take next.

The officer in charge of the squad, a youngish blond man named Tanner, wandered across to get a signature.

"Looks like you've had a busy night, Marshal Cade."

Cade signed the arrest docket and handed it back. "It's not over yet," he said.

"Nothing but a slave driver," Janek muttered from the shadows behind Cade.

Cade ignored him. He strode across to the cruiser and climbed in. "You coming, Buddy Rich?"

Janek dropped into the passenger seat, slipping the SPAS back in its cradle. He took a long look at Cade as he fired the cruiser out of the freight yard.

"Buddy Rich? You been holding out on me, T.J.? Don't tell me you're a jazz fan after all."

Cade only smiled, keeping his knowledge to himself. It would do Janek good to know he wasn't the only one with hidden depths. He also knew that his refusal to say anything further would really annoy his partner.

11

"What's our next move?" Janek asked as Cade rolled the cruiser into the basement garage under their apartment building. "As if I didn't know."

"So why ask?"

"I just want you to be sure you know what we're taking on, T.J."

"We?"

"You don't think I'd let you go to Lexus-9 on your own, do you? I couldn't sleep nights if I wasn't there to watch your back."

Cade stared at the cyborg. "To hell with what Milt Schuberg says, Janek. I think you're a nice guy."

"Cut it out," Janek replied, "you're embarrassing me."

"Now he starts getting embarrassed. What next—blushing?"

Cade cut the cruiser's engine. He sat still for a moment, scanning the garage. His attention suddenly focused on a particular vehicle.

"The black stretch limo," he said. "It doesn't belong here."

Janek unlimbered the SPAS, working a shell into the breech.

"Do we come out shooting, or wait until they show their hand?" he asked.

"Let's take it easy for now," Cade suggested. "I have a feeling somebody needs to talk to us. If they'd wanted us dead, they would have hit by now. And you don't use a gas guzzler like that for a quick getaway.''

"Smart thinking, T.J. You have the makings of a cybo in you."

"Heaven forbid," Cade said under his breath as he climbed out of the cruiser.

"I heard that," Janek told him. "If I was sensitive, I'd be hurt."

The limo's rear doors opened as Cade and Janek emerged from their car. Two men stepped from the dark interior. They were dressed alike, in dark suits. Each of them carried a suppressed Uzi 400. They placed themselves on either side of the limo, the autoweapons in full view but clearly meant more as a warning than a threat.

Cade sensed movement inside the rear of the limo.

"Detective Cade, a word if you don't mind."

The voice was low, well modulated. The tone suggested a man used to having his own way.

Cade crossed to stand a few yards from the open door of the limo. The interior of the car was in shadow, and Cade could only see the speaker's outline.

"Go ahead."

"You have been causing me some problems over the last few days. Because of your interference, I have lost valuable people and also money, and I resent those losses."

Cade suddenly understood that he was in the presence of Randolph Boon, the head of Lexus Incorporated, the man who was ultimately behind the Darksider hijackings, and also Kate Bannion's disappearance.

"It is time for it to stop, Cade," Boon went on. "There is too much at stake for me to allow you to carry on with all this nonsense."

"You have it wrong, Boon," Cade said. "I'm the one giving the warnings. It's you who's going to back off. Right now. The game's finished. I've got enough evidence to shut you down for good."

"Now that's what I like to hear!"

Cade turned and saw a figure stepping out of the deep shadows beyond the limo. It took him a few seconds to recognize the hard, gaunt features of Connor, the UCS captain.

"I admire a man who follows procedure," Connor said. "Gets all his evidence tagged and filed. Makes it a lot easier."

"They say when the ship starts to sink, all the rats come out of their holes," Cade remarked.

"Funny," Connor snapped. He flicked a hand.

The area was flooded with blinding light. Powerful beams glared harshly in Cade's face.

"I've got eight men tracked in on you, Cade. Believe me when I say they'll blow you into little chunks when I give the word. Let's have the piece on the floor. And tell your cybo buddy to do likewise. He can get it just the same."

Cade eased the Magnum from its holster and dropped it. Behind him Janek did the same with the SPAS and his own handgun.

"See how easy it is," Connor said. He planted himself in front of Cade. "You've been a regular pain in the ass since you called me the night Bernie Stenner fell into our hands. Hear me, asshole?"

Without warning, Connor drove his fist into Cade's stomach. Cade doubled over, gasping for breath. He felt Connor grab a handful of hair and yank his head up. He sensed the fist coming, but couldn't avoid it. The blow caught him across the right cheek, splitting the flesh as it snapped his head around. Grunting with the effort, Connor swung again and again, his fist connecting with Cade's face each time. Cade stumbled to his knees. Moments later Connor booted him in the side, sending him sprawling across the concrete. Cade had the sense to lie still, not wanting to provoke Connor's rage further. His face ached fiercely, and he could feel blood coursing down his cheek.

"Get him on his feet!"

Connor's voice came from a long way off. Rough hands hauled Cade upright. He leaned on their support.

"Nobody tells me to tighten up, Cade," Connor said, his face close to Cade's. "Not even a fancy badge from the goddamn Justice Department."

Shaking the mist from his eyes, Cade saw another face swim into view. Lean and well preserved, it gave the impression of inner hardness. The narrowed, cold eyes mirrored the man's soul.

"You've upset Mr. Connor rather badly," Randolph Boon said. "I can, of course, sympathize with him. Your intrusion into our affairs has upset a plan that was running very smoothly. Things have got away from us since you started interfering. We've had to take out some heavy insurance, but you've been the main problem, Cade. Chasing about the city, digging into every corner you can find and even going down to talk to the Darksiders. I can't say I'm all that concerned about you killing Rolf. That cretin was becoming an embarrassment. Granted, he was useful when it came to setting up the raids in the tunnels, but he was getting greedy. And then tonight's little fiasco over in Newark, Lasall being sent off in a police wagon. But despite your interference, I believe we can bring it all back under control once we have you removed from the scene. And Mr. Connor will have that carried out with his usual expertise."

"It won't end," Cade said. "Killing me doesn't stop the investigation. Somebody else will pick it up once they realize I've disappeared."

"You can't frighten me with tales about the Justice Department. Even they aren't infallible. By the time your disappearance has been registered, we will have engineered a thorough cover-up. This whole affair will have been fine-tuned so there won't be a thing to be found. You're not dealing with a disorganized street-gang, Cade. Over the years I've fostered special relationships with people in high places, people who can help me in times of trouble. You only managed to uncover the tip of the iceberg, barely worth raising a sweat over."

"You want me to tell him about Krask and company?" Connor asked, grinning from ear to ear.

"Why not?" Boon said. "Perhaps it will convince him I'm not talking nonsense."

"You figure you've got it made with Krask, Lasall and Lippin under lock and key? Witnesses who can talk and finger us all?" Connor chuckled. "Forget it, pal. They're fried by now, along with those local Newark cops. While you and the cybo were driving back from Newark, my people took out the wagon. Hit it with hand-held missiles, then laid in a couple of thermal shells. Burned the whole fuckin' crew to a crisp."

One of the men holding Cade upright said, "I guess you could say your buddy Tanner got his hide well tanned."

"You see, Cade, we are not playing games. The stakes are too high. I have enough invested in this deal that I can't allow you to ruin it," Boon said. "You should have stayed well out of it. But it's too late now."

"Okay," Connor snapped, "we're wasting time. Get them out of here. One of you follow with their cruiser. Dispose of that also. I want a total wipeout as far as this pair is concerned. I don't want a scrap of bone or a rivet left. Eddie, you know what to do. Give Mr. Boon and me time to get over to his place. We need to be in the crowd when you off this pair. And do it right. No mistakes.''

Cade watched Connor and Boon start walking away and waited a second, then yelled, "Connor!"

The man half turned back toward Cade, his head cocked.

"You're dead, Connor. You and Boon both."

Connor laughed out loud this time. "Coming from you, that's rich. What you going to do? Come back from the fuckin' grave and haunt me?"

Cade held the man's hard stare. He could taste blood in his mouth, and his right eye was beginning to swell over and close. "Whatever it takes, Connor. Believe me. You can bank on it."

Connor maintained his casual grin, but for a moment the defiant gleam faded from his eyes. Then he turned and walked on to the limo to climb in behind Boon. The doors slammed shut, and the vehicle moved off.

Cade watched it go. He was still watching it when someone hit him from behind, the blow crunching down across the back of his skull and pitching him into a void of swirling darkness.

"T.J.? CAN YOU HEAR ME?"

Cade opened his good eye, peering out on a scene that made him think he was already in hell.

The semidarkness appeared to be framed by a swell of boiling fire. The air was hot and stank of molten metal. In the background the thump of machinery matched the pounding inside Cade's skull.

"Thomas?"

"Yeah, I hear you," Cade said, wincing at the vibration his words created.

He felt Janek's hands on his shoulders, lifting him into a sitting position.

"Where the hell are we?"

"Somewhere in the South Bronx," his partner informed him. "A wrecker's yard. I get the feeling they intend disposing of us along with the cruiser."

Cade stared around him. He and Janek were secured inside a small steel cabin overlooking the main area of the yard. They were surrounded by piles of dilapidated and wrecked vehicles, everything from cars to massive diesel trucks. The vehicles had been dumped in the yard for smelting down. The recycled metal would be refined and used again.

The night sky over the yard reflected the glow of fire from the smelting pits, where the molten metal was collected after it had gone through the process. The dangerous work was carried out by machines controlled by computer, while menial tasks were done by workdroids.

The cabin Cade and Janek squatted in was open to the night sky. An armed man stood outside. The others were ranged in a loose group around the police cruiser, deciding who should take possession of the SPAS shotgun.

"How long have we been here?" Cade asked.

Janek thought for a few seconds. "Precisely twelve minutes, thirteen seconds."

"And what have you done about getting us out?"

Janek gave his lopsided shrug. "Me?" he asked.

"I figured while I was unconscious you might come up with something."

"Jack shit, actually," Janek admitted.

"Great," Cade said. "And since when did you take up swearing?"

"I figured it covered my feelings quite well."

"Well, let's just do something before they barbecue us."

"I didn't want to risk starting anything until you were conscious," Janek explained. "I was worried about you, T.J."

"Shut up in there," the guard said over his shoulder. He was irritated because he'd been made to watch the prisoners while the others argued over the SPAS.

"Go suck, pal," Cade replied. "You're going to kill me, remember? So why should I be quiet?"

"Kill you, sure. But I might just take the time to kick the stuffing out of you first!"

"You might at that, but only if you brought your mother along."

"Bastard," the guard said, rising to the bait. He turned and kicked open the door. Framed in the gap, he swung the muzzle of his Uzi in Cade's direction. "You want it now, cop?"

"If you've got the guts, twinkle-toes!"

The guard spit out an obscenity. He took another step inside the cabin, the Uzi tracking in on Cade's head.

"Now you've bought it!" the guard snarled.

He didn't see Janek move until it was too late. The cyborg uncoiled from his squat on the floor with a smooth powerful movement, left hand striking out and grabbing the Uzi. Janek's right hand closed around the guard's throat, his fingers exerting the kind of pressure that could buckle steel. The guard's neck snapped with a loud crunch, his limbs twitching awkwardly before Janek let him fall.

Cade scooped up the Uzi and flattened against the steel wall, unscrewing the suppressor and tossing it in the cor-

ner. He waited until his partner had armed himself with the
dead man's handgun. Janek also found spare clips for both
weapons in the man's coat. He tossed the Uzi clips to Cade.

"You set?" Cade asked.

Janek nodded, snapping back the autopistol's slide. "It's
every man for himself," he said, swinging the door open and
breaking into the open.

Cade followed on the cyborg's heels, breaking to the right
when Janek moved left.

The gunmen grouped around the cruiser were already reacting, weapons arcing around and spitting flame.

Janek fired on the run, his pistol rattling out shots with
unerring accuracy. His first volley took out two of Connor's gunmen, the heavy-caliber slugs tearing fist-sized holes
in their chests and hurling them across the rutted ground.

Closing in from the other side, Cade turned the Uzi loose,
and the 9 mm slugs drilled into their targets. Bodies were
sent sprawling across the ground, flesh erupting with crim-
son sprays, but Cade kept his finger on the trigger to scat-
ter the gunmen.

Return fire whizzed by, and Cade took a reckless dive,
skinning his left elbow as he hit the ground, then rolling
frantically. He banged up against a stack of auto tires, disturbing their precarious balance. The tires toppled to the
ground around him, bouncing and rolling in all directions.
Cade used the disturbance to scramble to his feet and duck
behind a gutted car body. Slugs whacked into the metal and
howled off into the night sky as he crouched in the dirt,
feeding a fresh clip into the Uzi.

Above the crackle of gunfire and raised voices, he picked
up the thump of running feet. They were nearing his hiding
place. Cade gripped the Uzi, trying to pinpoint the man's
position. There was a thump against the side of the car body

as the enemy gunman reached it then paused before moving on.

He dashed across Cade's line of vision, and Cade triggered the Uzi. The gunman seemed suspended in the air, twitching from the multiple impacts, then he crumpled to the ground to lie in a bloodied heap.

PUTTING ON a burst of speed, Janek found cover behind the dark, rust-streaked bulk of an old fuel tanker. He dropped to a crouch and peered under the chassis and caught movement on the far side as two of Connor's men reached the tanker. Without hesitation Janek leaned under the chassis, leveling the autopistol. He fired twice, putting bullets through one pair of legs, then switched aim and took out the second gunman. They toppled to the ground but still tried to track in on Janek. He fired twice more, shots that ended the moaning for good. The cyborg stood up and swung himself on top of the tanker's walkway. He found the metal ladder that curved up the side of the tanker barrel. When he reached the top, Janek stretched out full length, surveying the scene below.

There were only two of the gunmen left. They wore oily coveralls, identifying them as part of the crew from the wrecker's yard. One carried the SPAS, while the other was armed with an Uzi. They were still huddled beside the cruiser, scanning the area and trying to decide what to do. Janek helped them with their decision.

He tracked the guy with the SPAS, triggering a quick shot that took the gunman's head apart. As the dead man sprawled at his partner's feet, Janek loosed off another snap shot. The heavy slug caught the target in the center of his chest, coring through to blow out between his shoulders in a bloody spray. He flopped back against the side of the cruiser, leaving a red smear on the dirty paintwork as he slithered to the ground.

Janek made his way to the ground, then walked around the tanker and met Cade as he emerged from behind the burned-out car.

Janek picked up the SPAS and handed it to Cade.

"You want to get out of here?" Janek asked. "I'm starting to feel uncomfortable with all this scrap metal around me."

Cade grinned. "Keep this up, and you'll develop a sense of humor."

They settled in the cruiser, with Janek taking the wheel. He fired up the engine, then swung the car toward the gate.

"So?" he asked as he gunned the cruiser along the deserted street.

"The Heights," Cade said. "Let's go calling. I feel in the mood to crash a party. I want Boon and Connor behind bars before we go after Kate."

He picked up the handset and called into the NYPD, asking for Milt Schuberg.

"Hey, T.J., what trouble you in now?"

"Milt, listen. I'm at a wrecker's yard down in the South Bronx." Cade leaned out the window and read off the street name as they sped by an intersection.

"Yeah."

"Get a squad down here. I've left some DOAs for you. Then get your ass into gear and haul it over to the Heights. You heard of Randolph Boon, the industrialist? His place. He's the guy behind the problems I've been having. He's got a partner, too. Captain in the Urban Crime Squad. Name of Connor. You remember Connor? I'm on my way to pull them in right now."

"You sure know how to liven up a guy's evening."
Schuberg hesitated for a moment. "What the hell is this all
about?"

"I'll tell you later, Milt. Just do it."

"And don't stop to eat on the way," Janek said testily.

"Dammit, Cade, I'll screw the bolts off that tin man one
day. You listening, Janek? You trash-can reject!"

"So's your old man," Janek warbled.

"One thing, Milt. Run some checks, because you've got
a leak in your department. Boon's got someone on his payroll."

Cade switched off the handset and turned to Janek.
"Let's go, hotshot," he said, nursing his skinned elbow.
"Damn, it hurts," he grumbled. "How come this never
happens to TV cops when they do it?"

"They have the brains to use cybo stand-ins to do their
stunts for them," Janek said. "It's also why they earn a lot
more money than you do."

"Janek."

"Yes, T.J.?"

"Just drive the damn car."

12

"Before we go in, T.J., can I ask you a question?"

Cade was stuffing extra shells for the SPAS into his jacket pocket. He didn't reply directly. There was a distant, angry gleam in his unmarked eye. It was a look Janek had seen before and which he found unsettling.

He recognized his partner's mood. Cade himself would have described it as being really pissed off. Janek couldn't entirely condemn Cade's attitude. The cybo's partner looked decidedly the worse for wear. His face was showing the full effects of Connor's beating. His right eye was almost completely closed, and heavy, swollen bruises distorted his features. The gash over his right cheek was still bloody, with ragged edges to the split flesh. Cade's clothing, like Janek's, was crumpled from the episode in the wrecker's yard.

"If you expect me to tell you I'm going to read them their rights, don't hold your breath," Cade said. His words were carefully chosen, and delivered evenly and calmly.

Janek leaned back in his seat, gazing out through the cruiser's windshield. He felt sure he'd been through all this before with Cade—in fact, on more than one occasion. His own logic told him that Cade's attitude was a negative one, and in the cyborg's book that had to be wrong. Yet he was finding himself—and it was here that Janek's precise lines of logic became blurred around the edges—understanding and sympathizing with his partner's emotional decision.

"Can we at least give them the opportunity to surrender peacefully?" Janek asked patiently.

Cade took a deep breath, held it, then released it with a heavy sigh. "Just what do you think I'm going to do in there? Shoot everybody in sight?"

"You do have this tendency for the old gung-ho way of handling situations," Janek said in his most calming tone. "Probably because of your association with the Marines."

"That's just natural enthusiasm."

"My ass!" Janek snapped. "T.J., stop treating me like a rookie. I know what you're up to."

"Yeah?"

"Yeah," Janek mimicked. "To put it on your terms, you're all steamed up because of Kate, and Boon is going to get his butt caved in."

"Smart thinking."

Janek thumped his fist on the cruiser's dashboard. "Patronize me again, Thomas, and I'll . . ."

"You'll what? Haul off and slug me?" Cade snapped.

"Maybe I will."

"Try it for size, partner," Cade said, twisting around in his seat to glare at Janek.

There was a slight strained pause, and then Janek shrugged. "I wouldn't feel right about it," he admitted. "Shouldn't we be, er, working out our plan of action, T.J.?"

Cade relaxed and shrugged nonchalantly. "I guess so."

He fired up the cruiser and drove to the end of the elevated highway. It terminated in a covered parking area that allowed access to the elevator banks serving the luxury apartment complexes where Randolph Boon lived.

Cade and Janek were on Park Avenue Elevated-2, high above the city. They were in the heart of the Heights. The habitat of the ultrarich, the section of New York society that kept itself apart from the rest of the city. Here was Manhattan's wealth and power, the elite with the city's money and also its fate in their hands. It was said that there was more wealth in one apartment block in the Heights than in the rest of the city put together. Multiplied by all the residents of the area, it meant a total beyond imagination. It also meant it was forbidden territory. No one went into the Heights without invitation. Not unless they were looking for trouble.

The security protecting the Heights was not to be dismissed lightly. The guards who patrolled the walkways and plazas were known for their zeal and an uncompromising attitude toward any intruders. Trying to slip by security in the Heights was akin to suicide.

Cade climbed out of the cruiser and slammed the door shut. He walked across the open plaza, which was lush with sculptures and water fountains, heading for the access lobby.

Janek shook his head in resignation and fell into step behind Cade, scanning the area with both audio and visual modes.

A pair of uniformed security guards blocked Cade's path at the entrance to the softly lit access lobby. They had watched him approach, lounging with easy arrogance. Both wore heavy side arms on their hips.

"Hold it right there," one of them said as Cade closed in.

"Where do you think you're going?" the second man asked. He took a long look at Cade's battered face. "And what the hell happened to your face?"

Cade paused and looked the guards over casually. "Not tonight, boys," he said. "I've had enough shit to last me the rest of my life. So don't give me a hard time."

The first guard gave an ugly chuckle. "You've no idea what having a hard time means. Now shift your ass out of here before I zap you."

As he spoke he unhooked the electric prod on his belt. Grinning, he touched the button recessed in the handgrip, and blue sparks flashed between the electrodes at the business end of the stick.

"Wanna light up your day?"

"Go ahead if you figure you can reach me, lard-ass," Cade taunted.

His words drew the man out of the lobby entrance. The security man lunged at Cade, swinging the prod for a quick strike. Cade didn't budge until the last moment, then twisted to one side, feeling the crackling probes swish by. Then he brought his SPAS into play, slamming the barrel down across the guard's wrist. Bones snapped audibly, and the man yelled. Cade backhanded him with the SPAS, across the side of the head. The security man did an awkward belly flop. He bounced when he hit the concrete, then lay very still.

The moment he had hit the first guard, Cade had swung the SPAS, now held two-handed, to cover the second man. That guard had already made a grab for his gun, but when he saw the black hole of the SPAS staring at him he quickly put his hands up.

Cade reached over and took away his gun and stick, tossing them across the plaza. He stared at the guard.

"You son of a bitch," he said softly. "You were going to shoot me."

"I...I have a job—" the guard stammered. He didn't like the cold expression on Cade's face.

Cade passed the SPAS from his right to his left hand. Without warning, he threw a hard right that caught the unsuspecting guard across the side of his jaw. The force of the blow turned him completely around and laid him out flat on the concrete.

Janek reached Cade after he had disarmed and cuffed the first guard. He looked down at the second man, then at Cade, who was flexing his right hand and examining the bleeding skin of his knuckles.

"That hurt?"

Cade only nodded.

"Tough," Janek said tautly. He bent over and cuffed the guard Cade had slugged. "What was the point of that?"

"The mother was going to shoot me."

"I can understand how he felt," Janek said, and walked into the lobby.

The softly lit, expensively decorated lobby displayed a row of gleaming elevator doors. Randolph Boon had the rooftop complex. The elevator was operated by a coded access keypad, tied in to computer-controlled security.

"Can you override the sec-code?" Cade asked, stepping aside.

Janek stood by the keypad. He placed two of his fingertips against the com-link access pin and absorbed the code sequences, letting the information feed into his memory banks. He digested the electronic language, searched for and found the comparatively simple code and translated this into an override command. The elevator doors slid open.

"Sometimes, T.J., I amaze myself," Janek said smugly.

"I think I'm gonna throw up," Cade replied, and stepped inside the elevator.

Janek punched the button, and the doors closed. The elevator began its rapid ascent. One wall was transparent, allowing the Justice cops an unrivaled view of the city.

It spread before them with undiminished brightness, the shining towers and interconnecting highways ablaze with light. By day the city's grayness was laid bare, exposing its slow decline, but once the darkness shrouded the fading glory, New York took on a different look. The real city was lost in the shadows, replaced by the shimmering spectacle of the nighttime Babylon. It was a long-remembered image, no matter how false and self-deceiving.

"We're in the wrong business," Janek observed as he stared out across the glittering scene.

"What?"

Janek gave a tight grin. "We should be selling light bulbs."

Cade rolled his eyes but said nothing.

The elevator slowed, the indicator panel showing they had reached their destination. Before the car stopped completely and the doors opened, Cade and Janek moved to opposite sides, weapons up and ready.

The doors slid apart, revealing an opulent reception area and a trio of armed security men. The apparently empty car threw them off balance for a couple of seconds. One moved forward, peering into the car.

Janek struck from his side, and the barrel of his autopistol clubbed the guard across the back of the neck. The man silently flopped facedown on the elevator's thick carpet.

Cade shoved the barrel of the SPAS into view.

"Hold it," he said in a steely voice. "Don't make any moves."

One look at the ugly configuration of the combat shotgun convinced both men that it was not in their best interests to challenge Cade.

"Facedown," Janek ordered, and he quickly disarmed and handcuffed the guards.

Cade had already secured the unconscious man.

"I'm running out of cuffs," Janek stated.

Cade approached the double doors that would admit them to Boon's apartment complex.

"Boon and Connor are the ones we want," he said. "I don't know who else they may have in there to back them, so keep your eyes open."

Janek smirked. "One of us has to," he observed, "'cause you're no help."

Turning to the doors, Cade shoved them open and stepped inside the apartment's narrow but long foyer.

A wave of sound reached out to wash over him. Beyond the foyer was a vast room, its designed upper and lower levels filled with a crowd of elegantly dressed people. They stood in small groups or flitted back and forth. The murmur of their conversation and laughter all but overwhelmed the small musical combo playing on a raised dais. Weaving in and out of the crowd were half a dozen android waiters clad in immaculate white uniforms. They balanced trays of drinks and food with practiced ease, their presence unobtrusive and servile.

Cade watched the crowd, recognizing a number of well-known celebrities and local political figures among the expensively dressed and groomed guests.

Almost a full minute elapsed before someone noticed Cade's disheveled figure standing just inside the doorway. By then Janek had closed the doors and joined him, standing quietly with his back to the wall.

Cade's presence was quickly picked up by the assembled guests. The general buzz of conversation ebbed away, leaving only the music playing on, and even this faltered and ceased. Then Cade's shotgun was noticed.

"What's this all about?" a man demanded. "Do you realize where you are?"

"Where's Randolph Boon?" Cade asked.

"Who wants to know?"

Cade brought out his badge and held it up.

"Marshal Cade of the Justice Department. I'm only interested in Boon and Captain Connor of the UCS. The rest of you people stay out of my way, and I won't give you any hassle."

"You can't be serious," the man who had challenged Cade said. "This is Randolph Boon you're talking about, one of the city's most prestigious industrialists."

"I'm not interested in his pedigree," Cade stated flatly. "Right now he's the major suspect in an investigation, and I'm here to take him in."

"Marshal Cade, I'm Senator Griswald. I take exception to your intrusion here tonight, and I can assure you this matter will be taken to the highest authority. You've made a foolish move in coming here, one you might well regret."

Cade stepped in close to the senator.

"Save your breath, Senator. I don't melt into a greasy puddle when people make threats. If you want to join Boon, that's fine by me. If you don't, stand back and mind your own damn business."

Griswald's confusion showed in his eyes. He stared around him for support, but got none. There was almost relief in his expression when Randolph Boon's voice called out. "Is something wrong? Who told the band to stop...?"

Boon was pushing his way through the immobile guests when he spotted Cade. The industrialist froze.

"Boon, it was worth it just to see that look on your face," Cade said, and he meant every word. "Now get over here and stop pretending you don't know what's going on."

"Cade, I swear I'll see you walking a beat for this!"

Connor elbowed guests aside as he bulled his way through the crowd to stand next to Boon. "Get your ass out of here, Cade, or do you want me to call the mayor?"

"You mean the mayor isn't here?" Janek asked, making his presence known. "T.J., you told me Boon was important. It's not such a big bust after all."

Janek calmly marched up to Boon and took his arm.

"Let's go."

Connor swung around angrily, planting a thick hand against Janek's shoulder and attempted to push him off balance with a mighty shove.

"You had your chance earlier, Connor, and you lucked out," Janek said as he caught the captain by his collar and swung him effortlessly aside.

Connor stumbled across the floor, then reached for the gun he carried under his expensive jacket.

Cade took a long stride forward and rammed the SPAS's muzzle into Connor's stomach. Connor grunted, his weapon slipping from his hand. He lashed out at Cade and received a heavy backhander across his mouth in return, which sent him on a collision course with a table holding refreshments. Bottles and glasses crashed to the floor, and a gasp went up from the well-dressed crowd as they moved back to make room. Cade moved in for the kill, allowing himself a moment of satisfaction as he hit Connor a couple more times, driving the man back across the room. Gasping for breath, Connor went to his knees, his head down and blood dripping steadily from his split lips.

"On your feet, Connor," Cade said. "Don't give me another reason to pound the hell out of you. I don't need much."

Behind Cade a woman screamed, and he began to turn, sensing danger close by.

"T.J.! To your right—Jak Regis!"

Boon's hired killer.

Above the rising crescendo of screams and yells, Cade heard the savage rattle of an autoweapon.

Screams of fear turned to cries of pain as innocent guests were caught in the stream of fire, bullets ripping into vulnerable flesh.

Cade completed his turn, the SPAS already rising to firing level, his good eye searching desperately for the target.

He saw Regis on the far side of the room, standing in the doorway. The gunman was wielding a rapid-fire combat rifle, and even at a distance Cade could see the crazed gleam in Regis's eyes.

Just a few feet away Janek was pushing Randolph Boon to the floor and drawing his autopistol. Then he powered across the room, scattering guests before him, the powerful handgun seeking its target.

Regis loosed a final blast in Cade's direction before swinging the rifle at the approaching marshal.

"Janek! Watch yourself!" Cade shouted at his partner. He jammed the SPAS to his shoulder, finger easing back on the trigger.

Regis fired first, a short burst that caught Janek in the left chest and shoulder, spinning him off his stride and sending him down on his knees.

Then the SPAS exploded with sound, sending its deadly charge at Regis. The gunman twisted as the shot caught him in the left side just above the hip, and he staggered, falling against the door frame and bracing himself. He attempted to lift his rifle again, but Cade put two more shots into him. The first ripped into his arm, almost at shoulder level, shredding flesh and bone alike. Regis pulled the rifle's trigger, sending a sustained blast into the floor. He was lifted off his feet by Cade's final shot, the charge tearing his throat out in a bloody haze. Regis fell over backward, and the heels of his boots drummed briefly on the floor before being stilled.

Cade reached Janek's side as he got to his feet.

"You okay?" Cade asked.

Janek examined the ragged tears in his jacket and shirt.

"Well, these are beyond repair," he muttered. "But I suppose I can claim compensation from the department, T.J."

"Get real, Janek. Here I'm asking if you're okay, and all you can do is moan about your damn clothes."

Janek pulled aside the torn shirt and exposed his chest. His synthetic skin was punctured, showing a number of shallow dents in his titanium shell.

"I'll survive," he said.

Cade glared at him. "Glad to hear it, partner," he snapped. "Now let's get Boon and Connor dusted and ready for Milt when he arrives."

"Correction," Janek said, looking over Cade's shoulder. "Make that Boon on his own. Connor isn't going anywhere."

Cade turned. The UCS captain was sprawled on his back, eyes staring at the ceiling. There was a look of total surprise on Connor's face. His chest was a glistening mass of dark blood and torn flesh. Regis's final volley, intended for Cade, had instead taken out the crooked cop.

"WHEN YOU GO for it, T.J., the sky's the limit," Milt Schuberg remarked sourly.

The NYPD detective was surveying the mess the firefight had left behind. There were bullet holes in the walls and dark patches of drying blood staining the expensive carpet.

Regis's indiscriminate shooting had killed two of the guests and wounded five others. The casualties had been taken away by the paramedic team summoned by Cade, and the remaining guests had been moved to another room in the apartment complex for questioning by Schuberg's staff.

Randolph Boon was held in an isolated room, under close police guard.

"All I wanted was to make an arrest," Cade said. "Regis decided to make things hot."

"Yeah, yeah, I know," Schuberg groused. "Look, I think it's time you leveled with me. Just what has been going on the last few days?"

"I think it's time you told him," Janek said, glancing up from inspecting the rips in his clothing.

"He's right," Schuberg insisted, glad of an ally. "Hey, Janek, you should claim for that through the department."

"Don't you start, Milt," Cade growled. "He hasn't quit moaning since it happened."

Schuberg had helped himself to a slice of cold chicken from the buffet table and was now busily stuffing it into his mouth.

"Quit stalling, T.J.," he mumbled around a huge mouthful.

Cade gave him the whole story, from the time he'd picked up Bernie Stenner, then brought him up to date with the attempt to make himself and Janek disappear in the wrecker's yard and the confrontation at Boon's apartment.

"Hell, it has to be true because nobody could make up stuff like that." Schuberg shook his head as he absorbed the enormity of Cade's charges against Boon. "Can you make this stick? Let's face it, pal, you don't have many witnesses. And Boon is going to deny it all.''

"I've got all the facts and figures in here," Janek said, tapping the side of his head. "The cash transactions alone will go a long way to convict the man."

"But we're not dealing with street riffraff here," Schuberg pointed out. "Boon has a lot of contacts. Powerful people. You met one of them tonight. Senator Griswald. Boon can call in a lot of favors, Cade, and he will."

"So can I," Cade said, "but do something for me, Milt. Book the son of a bitch and make it hard for him to get bail."

"My pleasure," Schuberg said. "Hey, what about Kate? Look, pal, I know how you two fit together. I hope she comes out of this okay."

"So do I. Milt, I'm going to make this thing stick. Boon's not walking away free and clear."

"You figure on producing witnesses?"

"Yeah. It's going to take a while, but I have a feeling I can do it."

"Things could get sticky for you around here. You figuring on leaving town, T.J.?"

"A lot farther than that, Milt," Cade answered. "A hell of a lot farther."

13

Janek turned from the viewport, away from the black void of outer space with its sprinkling of stars, and faced the lean, earnest features of the U.S. Marine.

"Major Bronson sends his compliments, Detective Janek, and asks if you'd like to join him on the flight deck."

Janek nodded pleasantly and followed the young Marine, who wore the full uniform of the Space Corps, through the narrow companionways.

Around him the ship pulsed with contained power. Janek could sense the enormous potential within the sleek craft's fuselage. He was more in tune with the vessel than its human personnel. The cyborg's machine vibes responded in sympathy to those of the spacecraft.

Like its sister ships in the Marine Space Corps, the *Nui Vu* was named after an outstanding campaign in the Corps' history. Back in 1966, during the Vietnam War, a small contingent of Marines fought a classic battle against overwhelming odds—and won. The *Nui Vu* honored the battle and the men who took part.

The *Nui Vu* was a pursuit ship of the Suribachi Class, barely four years old. Powered by twin Pratt & Whitney nuclear fusion engines, it was capable of the highest speeds yet achieved in deep space. The product of long research, its engines derived their terrific thrust via fusion reactors fueled by helium 3 that came from the moon's unlimited supply. Helium fusion reactors, though well developed, had been held back from full use until intense lunar production of the element became a reality. Previous to this break-through the standard drive for deep-space craft had been the efficient but comparatively slow ion drive. The emergence of nuclear fusion engines had opened up the far frontiers of space for future explorers.

At present only the U.S. Marine Space Corps had opted for the NF-drive. They were quickly finding that the power gave them a distinct advantage over conventionally pow-ered craft.

Ducking his head as he reached the hatchway, Janek en-tered the flight deck. He was immediately impressed by the unhurried efficiency of the area.

As expected, the flight deck was a wonderland of tech-nology and electronic sophistication. Every bulkhead and space was crammed with consoles and instrument banks. Glowing readout screens threw subdued light across the flight deck. There was little sound, nothing more than a low electronic hum accompanied by the soft clicks of respond-ing machines.

On the far side of the flight deck, Cade was in deep con-versation with Major Bronson, the *Nui Vu*'s commander. Bronson was a tall, tanned Texan who spoke slowly and quietly. He was a career Marine and had earned his rank through serving in a number of global hot spots. Now he was working deep space. His main task was patrolling the traffic lanes between the Earth's orbit platforms and the Asteroid Belt. His brief was to maintain order and keep an eye open for illegal cargo runners.

Janek joined his partner, nodding at Bronson.

"What do you think of her?" the Marine asked. His pride in the *Nui Vu* showed in his tone.

"A fine ship, Major."

"According to the computer, we should easily be able to make up lost time. *Lexus-6* might have a few days' head start, but those Mitsubishi ion-drive engines are no match for us. Those ore freighters aren't built for speed. Just dependability."

Cade glanced at his partner.

"We've got some time to kill," he said. "You have any ideas?"

Janek smiled. "There's a great selection of music tapes on board," he said. "Including a lot of jazz tracks I haven't heard. So I'm going to be fine, T.J."

"Couple of my crew are into jazz in a big way," Bronson said. "What about you, T.J.?"

Cade stroked his bruised face. "A few days in the solarium might help. First thing I'm going to do is get a good meal inside me, then hit the sack. Catch up on some sleep."

"Marine training showing through." Bronson grinned. "Eat and sleep when you can, because you don't know how far off the next chance might be."

Leaving Janek to have a detailed look around the flight deck, Cade followed Bronson back to the recreation area, where they got themselves coffee and sat down.

"Glad we could help you on this, T.J.," Bronson said.

"Always helps having clout when an emergency comes up."

"Colonel McClain nearly did a back flip when you called him. He practically put the whole damn fleet on standby. Way I heard, you two go back a way."

Cade nodded. "We served in the same outfit. Had our best time during the '34-to-'36 war. McClain was heading for the top back then."

"You made yourself a reputation during the war," Bronson reminded Cade.

"We had a job to do," Cade replied. "We did it. Mind, here were some hairy times."

"Hairy? Mild way of talking about the raid on the Islamic Federation's nuke facility. If you guys hadn't put the place out of action, we might have had more than those chemical missiles landing back home."

Cade emptied his coffee cup. "Wild times," he reflected, almost as if he were alone, and there was a trace of regret for past glories in his tone.

"When we reach Platform-12, you and Janek make your landing by hired cruiser," Bronson said. "I'll stand by and wait for your call to come on in. We're monitoring all communications with the Asteroid Belt. If we hear anything that might be a warning to Lexus-9, we jam it. Problem with somebody like Randolph Boon is his connections. You might have the main man under lock and key, but how many more are there on his payroll?"

"At least my contact on the NYPD latched on to the leak in his department. The guy was in the communication section, so he had an ear open for anything coming in that might involve Boon's organization," Cade said. "I'm hoping we got to the main people in time. I don't want to get to Lexus-9 and find all the Darksiders have been buried underground somewhere because someone knew we were coming."

"The one they ought to bury is that bastard Boon," Bronson said, allowing his professional mask to slip for once.

"He isn't getting away with this," Cade said. "I've already made that promise."

"Are you sure you don't want immediate backup?" Bronson asked. "You only have to say the word."

Cade shook his head. "Just Janek and me. I want to ge to them before they know what's hit 'em. Too many bodie could give the game away. The things I have to do I can d best on my own. Just you keep your ear to the radio and come running when I give the word."

Bronson nodded. He knew about Cade's personal stake in the venture and admitted the logic of the Justice cop' approach.

"We won't let you down," he promised.

Cade stared at him. "Hell, Bronson, that never ever crossed my mind."

He stood up, stretching tiredly. The effects of the pas days were really catching up now. He felt dog tired, bruised and battered. Even the past few hours, with the drive to the Newark shuttle port and the transfer from earth to Orbi Platform Pegasus-2, where he and Janek had been met by Bronson and escorted to the *Nui Vu,* had been intense. Ad justing to the shuttle flight and the blast-off from the plat form had drained the last of Cade's energy. He was ready for a good meal and then sleep. After that he would face whatever lay ahead.

And hoped he would still be in time to find Kate be fore...

Before what?

Cade decided he didn't want to pursue that line of thought. Not yet.

14

Time passed with agonizing slowness for Kate Bannion. The trip to Lexus-9 seemed to be taking forever. The problem was her isolation from anything she could relate to. Although she had been allowed out of her cell after the first week, accompanied by the android that brought her food, Kate's contact with other occupants of the freighter was minimal and when it did happen the meetings were less than satisfactory.

Her short stretches of freedom gave her opportunity to take showers and have her clothes cleaned and returned. It was only after the third visit to the shower that she realized she was being watched. The android, who accompanied her everywhere, and who even stood by as she took her showers, caught her attention. Kate became aware that the robot's close scrutiny of her actions was more than just casual. She realized that the android's amber eyes were taking too much in. Especially when she realized it was focusing on certain parts of her anatomy.

A cold shiver ran through her, despite the heat of the water spraying her body. The android was recording her taking a shower. It was being manipulated from elsewhere on the freighter. Someone was using the android's vision, coupled to a vid-recorder, to get her on tape. With great self-control Kate carried on showering, her body reacting to the thought that she was being seen by human eyes. She could have shown her feelings in anger, or even embarrassment, but she wasn't going to allow them the pleasure of seeing her squirm. Instead she completed her shower, dried herself, then dressed.

She strode up to the android and confronted it.

"If I was you, I'd give up that bad habit," she said defiantly. "Too much staring at naked ladies will make you go blind."

She turned on her heel and walked back to her cell.

The android's voyeurism continued each time Kate showered, but she could handle it now. The knowledge that her unseen audience had been caught out took the edge off the practice, and Kate didn't even think about it any longer.

The problem with being isolated meant she had plenty of time on her hands. Kate used it to make decisions about what she would do when she reached Lexus-9. Whoever was controlling her life would have to decide what was going to happen to her. It had occurred to Kate that her death might not be imminent. If they had wanted her dead, why go to all this trouble? She could have been killed back in the underground tunnels when Rolf had caught her, or she could have been dumped in space during the trip to Lexus-9. Maybe they were keeping her alive so she could be questioned about her Darksider investigation. Not that she had much to tell. True, she had established Lisa's story about Darksiders being hijacked. That part was no secret. What she hadn't figured yet was where the tunnel dwellers were being taken. She felt she had an answer in part. Kate felt certain that if she checked the freighter out she would find Darksiders on board.

She knew that Lexus-9 was part of Lexus Incorporated, the mining division. Her agile mind tossed the facts back and forth until she came up with the only explanation that sounded right. Mines were dark, underground places. The Darksiders lived below the surface in dark, underground places. Mines plus Darksiders? Workers for the mines? It was all she could come up with, and it sounded logical. Dredging up all she could about the Asteroid Belt mining operations, Kate recalled that despite machine advances, mining was still an occupation best suited to the adaptability of human workers. It was hard, backbreaking work, and the mines were dangerous, inhospitable places. The men who worked in them were a special breed. Tough, courageous men who accepted the risks for the high wages they earned. But the Darksiders were not miners, nor were they experienced. So it didn't make a lot of sense for them to go down into the lonely tunnels where inexperience could add up to a high death rate.

She thought long and hard over that part of the puzzle. Why would Darksiders be used to replace skilled miners?

Because they were plentiful according to the numbers taken. Easily replaceable if they died off.

Something struck a chord in her mind. How would the contracted miners react to Darksiders being worked alongside them? The answer was simple. They wouldn't know about it. The miners had a strong union. It would refuse to allow unskilled workers alongside its members. So the Darksiders would be used in a part of the mine away from the regular work force, someplace where the miners themselves might refuse to work. A location that was so dangerous the union men would refuse to go in. A faulty section? Liable to cave-ins? Something illegal?

A rich seam in a dangerous corner of the mine. Maybe one that had been posted off-limits.

So the only way to work it was to ship in helpless Darksiders. Work them till they dropped, then replace them.

The conclusion of her deliberations scared Kate. If the people who held her captive were as ruthless as that, then she wasn't going to cause them any grief.

The fear she felt was quickly pushed to the back of her mind. She was still frightened, but that was good because it kept her on her toes. That apart, Kate maintained her self-control with the thought that as long as she remained alert there was a chance she might come out alive. She felt safe in the knowledge that she would remain unharmed until she actually reached Lexus-9. Her captors would want to find out how much she knew and whether she had passed any of her information to other parties. Her usefulness would cease once they established her story. Until then she had to fight for time. She would have to watch for her chance, keep her eyes open for any help on the asteroid. Lexus-9 was a company rock, but Kate refused to believe that everyone there was in on the conspiracy. If she could contact someone who would listen, then she might get herself some help. And wasn't it true that the U.S. Marine Space Corps was around the Asteroid Belt? They were there to maintain the peace.

There was also the slim chance that the NYPD might start to look for her once she failed to report back to the newspaper. Jerry Konsaki would file a missing-person report eventually. But would the local cops do much about it? They were overworked and under a great deal of pressure. And would they even bother about going down into the tunnels? If they did, the Darksiders might not cooperate. Unless Lisa was found.

Maybe. Perhaps. If only.

Even if something was done, it could easily be too late. Time was slipping away, and if Kate had judged things correctly, time was something she didn't have the monopoly on.

KATE ATE AND SLEPT, exercised and slept some more. She sat out her solitary existence, filling the long hours with memories of her life. Friends. The important events. The good and the bad times.

She also thought about Cade a lot, mostly when she was on her bunk, in the darkness, drawing comfort from the shadows.

Thomas Jefferson Cade.

Most people saw him as a hard, uncompromising lawman with little time for anything but his work. Kate knew better. She would be the first to admit that when he carried his Justice badge he gave everything he had to the job—which he had to if he wanted to survive. Away from the violent, decaying streets of the city he showed another side to his nature. A side few ever saw.

He could be a stubborn, argumentative individual if the need arose, and throughout their relationship they'd had some stormy times. But she had never once found him to be anything but honest and sincere. He wasn't the kind to lie or cheat. Those faults didn't exist as far as Cade was concerned. He couldn't be petty or jealous, but he could be warm and understanding and loving.

Those were the qualities that drew Kate to him and kept her there. Right now she would have forgiven him anything just for him to be at her side. She needed his strength. His resolve.

Most of all she needed him to hold her.

His image danced before her eyes as she lay in her lonely bunk, the future before her highly precarious, and the past the only certain thing.

"COME WITH ME, Miss Bannion," the amber-eyed android said.

"Why?"

"We will be docking at the Lexus facility, Orbit Platform-12 in the next few minutes. I have been asked to escort you to the airlock. I hope your trip has been satisfactory."

Kate bit back any reply. She couldn't blame the android. It was only a machine carrying out the program fed into its memory chips.

She followed the chrometal robot through the endless companionways, down through the various deck levels until they reached the main airlock. Just as they reached it, Kate felt a slight nudge as the freighter locked on to the magnetic buffers of the docking bay. A deep, echoing thump rang through the hull as the docking bay's transit tunnel secured itself over the airlock. The hum of the electro-clamps releasing was followed by the soft hiss of air. Then the airlock began to open.

Kate looked around and found the android had gone. For a moment elation flowed through her, but hard fingers clamped over her arm. Kate turned and looked into the face of a stranger.

"Let's go," the man said. He urged her forward. "Don't play games with me. If I have to I'll kill you on the spot."

Kate didn't doubt his word. She noticed that he wore a handgun under his leather jacket.

As they walked through the tunnel and into the brightness of the transit lounge, he grinned at her.

"I enjoyed the showers best before you figured out what was happening. Used to be the crew's daily highlight. Pity you caught on. You didn't give such a lively show once you knew you were bein' watched."

"Nice to know somebody had an entertaining trip," Kate replied.

The man kept grinning. "You keep up that feisty spirit. Be useful where you're goin', honey. Believe me, it really will."

Kate wondered what he meant. The words puzzled her, and she was still debating their meaning when the shuttle from Platform-12 made touchdown at the main landing strip on Lexus-9.

15

Cade and Janek had joined Bronson in the officer's club at the Marine Space Corps' facility on Platform-12. They had a couple of hours to kill while the shuttle they had hired was readied for them. The *Nui Vu* was docked and undergoing a thorough service check, which meant that Bronson and his crew were off duty for a while. The Marine major's first request was for Cade and Janek to join him for a celebratory drink.

The Texan grinned, raising his glass of Southern Comfort. "We did it, guys. We cut over two days off the record. Now you tell me the *Nui Vu* isn't a great ship."

"I was wrong to doubt you, Bronson," Cade admitted. "That was one hell of a trip."

"Tell the truth, boys, I've been waiting for an excuse to push those engines to the limit."

Bronson was still grinning as he downed his glass and immediately refilled it.

"Will it cause any lasting damage?" Janek asked.

"To the ship or my career?" Bronson asked, peering across the rim of his glass at Janek. "Hell, even Marine majors have to bend the rules once in a while. Anyhow, she was in a good cause."

"The arrest of Randolph Boon's accomplices?" Janek said.

"No, dammit, to save a lady's honor," Bronson told him. "T.J., it doesn't take the brains of a mule to see this partner of yours wasn't built in the state of Texas."

"To tell the truth," Cade said, "I'm convinced he popped out of the toaster one day."

Chuckling softly, Bronson stared at the cyborg. "Why, he's a solemn old boy, isn't he, T.J.? Pity they didn't design him so he could down a shot of this here golden nectar. Now, that would loosen up his joints."

Janek watched his two human companions, and a grunt of disapproval passed his lips. "If you two carry on the way you are, 'loose' won't be the word," he said sternly.

"Watch out, T.J., the party pooper's on to us."

"Having Janek around is like hauling your conscience behind you."

"In your case it's a waste of effort," Janek said. "I'll go take a look and see if the shuttle's ready."

Then he got up and left the bar.

"We haven't offended him?" Bronson asked.

"Janek? No way. He's a hardass," Cade said, but at the back of his mind he couldn't shrug off the odd look he'd seen in his partner's eyes.

Janek was his old self when Cade and Bronson joined him later at the shuttle bay. Janek pointed out the ship they would be using. It was a standard shuttle, thirty feet long, and ugly. The shuttle's outer shell was scarred and filthy. Its appearance took away all the romance about space travel. The shuttle's sole purpose was to ferry people down from the orbit platform to the asteroids, in this instance Lexus-9. The trip would take just over three hours.

Bronson handed Cade a lightweight pack. Inside was the Marine-issue transmitter that Cade could use to summon Bronson's assistance when he needed it.

"Once you get the goods on our boys, you hit that panic button and we'll get to you fast," Bronson said. "After you blast off, I'm moving a squad into orbit above Lexus-9. The minute we catch your signal, we can be down in under half an hour. Make sure you carry those miniature tracking devices at all times. Once you activate them, we can home in.''

Bronson followed them to the transit tunnel belonging to the shuttle-rental company and wished them good luck.

Janek had the paperwork all signed. He'd paid the rental fee with a credit card issued by the Justice Department, which identified the two of them as equipment salesmen. Both Cade and Janek carried paperwork to that effect. The company they were supposed to represent was entirely fictitious but was covered by a Justice Department setup on Earth.

Once they were on board the shuttle, Janek took over the controls. His memory store fed him the information he required to handle the craft, and he eased away from the docking bay as though he'd been piloting shuttles all his life.

Cade checked out the pack Bronson had given him. The transmitter, complete with a long-life power pack, was compact and sturdy. If the power pack failed, the transmitter had a backup solar-energy absorber. In fact the absorber reacted to any form of light. It would draw power from an artificial light source. The tracking devices were coin-sized disks with a wide-ranging signal and had enough power to transmit for at least fifty hours.

''Here,'' Cade said, handing over one of the devices. ''And don't lose it.''

''I won't.'' Janek took the tracker and slipped it into his pocket.

''You okay?'' Cade.

''Fine, T.J.,'' Janek replied, though he failed to convince his partner.

"Spit it out, Janek," Cade said. "You don't fool me. Something's bugging you. Come on, partner. Like you always tell me, don't hide your feelings."

"But I'm only a machine, T.J. A cyborg. Machines don't have feelings. Do they?"

Cade dropped into the copilot's seat. He watched as Janek did a thorough instrument check, then punched in the course for Lexus-9.

"I thought we knew each other better than that. You're my partner. I don't go around consciously thinking about the fact that you're a cybo."

"You bawl me out when you get angry."

"So? Do you think it would be different if you were human? Any partnership is based on a mix of emotions. It's like Kate and me. You've heard us row. Everyone has a different personality, and at times those differences clash. So people strike out verbally. It gets the frustration out of the system. It doesn't mean one person hates the other. It's part of the relationship. It's ongoing, Janek. It isn't something static. Emotions like love and understanding and tolerance develop with time."

"It gets confusing for me sometimes, T.J."

Cade grinned. "You and me both. We all have that problem."

"But I'm programmed to approach things logically. Emotion doesn't come into it." Janek hesitated. "Only I've been experiencing *feelings* lately, T.J., and I don't understand them."

"You remember Dr. Landers at Cybo Tech? I had the same conversation with her. Janek, I think what you're experiencing is an expansion of your intelligence toward human emotions. It's a natural progression of your programming development. You were created to simulate human behavior so you could function within society. Okay, you've gone one step further. Instead of just analyzing your reactions, you are automatically responding. Because you actually feel those emotions."

Janek turned to look directly at Cade. "You know what you're saying, don't you? There are people who wouldn't take kindly to a cyborg with humanlike emotions."

Cade shrugged. "So we don't tell anyone. We keep it between ourselves."

"You'd do that for me? Conceal it?"

"Like I said, Janek, we're partners. And partners look out for each other."

"Yes," Janek said softly.

"Mind, I still get to call you names if you piss me off."

This time Janek smiled. "I understand, T.J. Only promise me one thing. If we have a big argument, don't ever do what you do when you and Kate make up."

"You can bet your tin ass on that, partner."

LEXUS-9 LAY BELOW THEM. Janek had the shuttle in orbit above the dark, bleak surface of the asteroid. He had locked on to the landing marker and was punching in the autopilot codes.

There were a number of spacecraft already in the area. Huge ore freighters, their massive bulk overshadowing the tiny shuttle, slid silently by. There were smaller craft, other shuttles, fuel freighters and service ships belonging to numerous companies and supplying goods and services to the asteroid's business and pleasure facilities. There were even a number of sleek, privately owned cruisers.

"Shuttle 204," came the voice of the controller from the landing complex. "Your landing coordinates have been cleared and logged in. Permission to break orbit. And have a good flight in.''

"Confirmed," Janek answered. "Better strap in, T.J."

The shuttle automatically made a short burn, altering its position, then fired its motor again to give it the needed thrust. Cade and Janek, strapped into their couches, were able to view the asteroid's approach as the shuttle curved in toward the surface.

"Let's hope the communication blanket worked," Cade said. "If it hasn't, we'll be walking right into Boon's hired guns."

Janek tapped his titanium body through his clothing. "Yes, sometimes I'm glad to be a cyborg," he said. "Did you forget to bring your body armor, T.J.?"

"You know how to stretch a friendship," Cade said.

Panel readouts flashed as the shuttle's on-board computer began to monitor their progress. The vid-screens rippled with figures and course patterns. The hum and click of the machinery filled the cabin.

Cade felt the sudden increase in weight as the retro-ports blew, slowing the shuttle's descent. The craft arced, rolling slightly as it settled to its final approach.

Through the shuttle's viewport Cade saw the landing site. It was a huge complex, capable of handling the largest freighter belonging to Lexus. The complex had been designed in the form of a huge wheel, with the control-and-passenger terminal situated within the central hub. The spokes of the wheel were the landing bays, each with its own docking facility.

The shuttle sank toward the landing bay it had been allocated, linked by computer to the dock. Guided in by the programmed machine, the shuttle nosed along the spoke of the bay until it came to rest. The craft settled with a hiss of hydraulic rams. Immediately the dock pushed out the transit tunnel, making an airtight seal and automatically releasing the electro-clamps on the shuttle's airlock.

"Docking completed. Passengers may disembark," control informed them.

Cade and Janek left the shuttle and walked down the transit tunnel. They emerged in the passenger terminal and made their way to the shuttle-rental counter where Janek completed the paperwork.

"I hope you will use us on your return trip," the android clerk said blandly.

"No personality to those Model 15s," he muttered as he rejoined Cade.

They wandered across the brightly lit terminal building. The place was wide and roomy. It had two tiers of shopping and restaurant galleries. The curved top was transparent. The ground level dealt with the mundane business of embarking and disembarking passengers. There were vidphone facilities and information booths. Cade and Janek located the access to the subway link. An automatic dispenser took their money and issued them tickets.

"It's like being back in New York," Cade grumbled, shouldering his personal holdall and pushing through the barrier.

"Hardly," Janek observed as they reached the platform. "No graffiti, T.J."

The sleek train slid into the station minutes later. Cade found a seat, but Janek wandered through the car, staring at the advertising posters and watching the TV monitors mounted in each section. They pumped out an endless display of ads and video programs.

"Same old junk," he said, settling beside Cade. "That cop show has been running in New York for the past three seasons."

"You can always depend on TV to keep everything the same."

Fifteen minutes later the train stopped at Lexus Central. Cade followed the arrows and took the escalators to the main concourse, with Janek trailing behind him. The cyborg's eyes were everywhere, taking in his new surroundings.

Lexus City was made up of a series of huge domes linked by sealed tunnels and underground passages. Although Lexus had claimed the asteroid as its own with regard to the mineral rights, Washington Central was still the administrator, and the asteroid remained under federal jurisdiction. It had been decided to bring the asteroids under Washington's control after the early, bloody wars between the emerging mining consortiums. A situation had developed that closely resembled the days of the range wars back in the 1800s, with greedy individuals attempting to gain control of the rich asteroids. Cade had been in the thick of the troubles during his hitch with the Marine Space Corps, and Lexus had been one of the worst hot spots.

Things had changed for the better while he'd been away. Lexus City had developed into an established community that resembled an Earth city, apart from its being housed beneath a series of vast, transparent domes.

"We'll find a hotel and get ourselves settled," Cade said. "Then we start."

16

There were four major domes making up the greater part of Lexus City. In these were the financial, administrative and white-collar residential areas. Included in the largest dome were hotels and up-scale leisure shopping malls. Lexus City was looking to the future as interest in deep-space pleasure cruising grew. Six smaller domes comprised the outer zone, catering to the housing-and-entertainment needs of the mine workers. Two of the domes housed industrial units and storage facilities. Beyond Six Domes, as the workers' area had been named, stood the towering block of the nuclear reactor that provided power for the asteroid. The reactor fed the city and also the sprawling mine complex of Lexus-9 farther to the north.

Cade and Janek hired a car to take them the ten miles from their hotel to Six Domes. The sleek vehicle, powered by electricity, took them through the access tunnels, some of which were underground, while other sections were located above the surface of the asteroid. They could have gone by subway, but Cade liked the idea of being independent when it came to moving about. It was also easier to transport the transmitter by car.

The closer they got to Six Domes, the more certain Cade became that they were doing the right thing. The Darksider problem was linked with the actual production side of Lexus-9, so it was within the mine complex that they would need to concentrate their probe.

They reached Six Domes close to nine, evening time. The asteroid operated on a schedule based on Earth time in order to balance the artificial light required at all times. Adjustments were made to imitate dawn and dusk.

Checking the computer readout on the car's vid-screen, Janek was able to bring them into the industrial area, close to the access roads that led into the actual mine complex. He swung into the parking lot of a deserted diner and cut the power.

"Plan of action?" he asked.

"I don't see any other way than going in and forcing their hand," Cade said. "Asking polite questions isn't going to get us a damn thing. These people are running an illegal operation. We can't afford to give them any chance to get rid of the evidence. Agreed?"

Janek nodded. "On this particular occasion, I'm inclined to go with you. Can I mention something?"

"Go ahead," Cade said. He was unzipping the holdall he'd brought with him. From it he produced the stripped-down SPAS he'd lugged with him from New York.

"We have two objectives. The locating and release of the Darksiders. And finding Kate."

"I know," Cade said in a tight voice. "I feel torn, tugged in two directions. But Kate…Kate is a victim here…a victim who is punished because, true to form, she wanted to help others. So who counts more, this single person I love, or a hundred others?"

"You are getting yourself stuck in an emotional quandary," Janek told him. "And there is no need to make the kind of choice you are considering, not while we are both around."

"What are you suggesting, Janek?"

"We separate. One goes into the mine complex and handles the Darksiders. The other returns to Lexus City and looks for Kate."

Cade's face lightened somewhat, but he concentrated on locking the SPAS together, then he loaded the weapon.

"You want to toss for it?" he asked, still trying to be fair and objective.

"No," Janek said. "I'll go into the mine. You go look for Kate."

"You sure?"

"You've got her on your mind. Without meaning to, you might allow it to cloud your judgment. And that could get you killed. I wouldn't like that to happen."

"Thanks, pal."

"I was thinking—if you got killed, I'd have to break in a new partner."

Cade just stared at him, not quite sure how to take the remark. For a few seconds he believed Janek meant it, then he caught the faint smile on Janek's lips.

A moment later Janek began to laugh. It began as a gentle chuckle, then rose until he was emitting a full-blooded, belly-shaking laugh.

Cade found himself grinning, not as much at the fact that his partner had laid one on him, but because Janek had found it amusing.

"Glad you found it funny."

Janek had sobered and was looking slightly embarrassed. "It was the look on your face, T.J. It was . . ."

"Something else for you to figure out, friend. What makes people laugh and why." He patted Janek's shoulder. "It's hell being human."

After climbing out of the car, Janek peeled off his outer clothing and pulled on a one-piece jumpsuit. He slipped on his shoulder holster, checking that his autopistol was fully loaded. He placed extra clips in the suit's zip pockets. The small tracking device went into the top pocket.

"While we were on Platform-12, I ran a check through the Marine Corps' main computer. I accessed information regarding Lexus freighters coming in from Earth. Only one has made the outward journey within the time scale, and according to the computer it's still in dock. It could be a good starting point for you. You need to look for *Lexus-6*."

"How about you?" Cade asked.

Janek picked up the transmitter. "I'll be fine. Trust me."

"I do," Cade replied, powering up the car and reversing across the lot.

Janek watched him disappear from sight along the road leading back to Lexus City. He slung the transmitter from his shoulder by the strap and slipped into the shadows.

CADE LEFT THE CAR near the entrance to the port complex and made his way inside. He was armed with his .357 autopistol, holstered under his leather jacket. Following the indicator signs, he headed for the freighter section. This was on the far side of the complex, away from the passenger terminal.

After a while he found his way barred by a closed gate. He walked on by, continuing along the same passage. The place was fairly quiet at this time of night. He reached a secondary passage that was signed, Restaurant Access—Administration Staff Only. Cade took the passage. It led to automatic doors that allowed him to enter a self-service cafeteria. He saw that there were only two people in the place, seated at a table on the far side. He walked across to the long, shiny counter and helped himself to a cup of coffee from a dispenser. The other customers didn't even look up from their conversation. Making his way to a table, Cade spotted a door that led through to the kitchens. He sat down near them and waited.

A few minutes later a pair of workdroids came in from the kitchens. They were armed with cleaning equipment. They started at the far end of the long room, cleaning the floor and also the tables.

The two customers in conversation finished their drinks and left as the workdroids neared their table. The moment they had left, Cade finished his coffee, stood up and walked to the kitchen doors. He went through.

The gleaming, silent kitchen was deserted except for a number of domestic androids preparing food. One glanced up as Cade approached. Before it could speak, Cade took out his wallet and flashed his Justice marshal badge.

"Health department spot check."

"No one told me," the android complained.

Cade smiled. "Wouldn't be a spot check if they did, would it?"

The android digested the logic, then nodded.

"You in charge?"

"Yes, sir."

Cade checked the ID number on the android's torso. "Fine, 5344-D. You're doing a good job."

The android perked up. "Thank you, sir. We try to maintain a high standard."

"I need to drop in on the freight-servicing bays. See if they're as alert as you. Can I get through from here?"

The android led him through the kitchen to a side door.

"Follow the passage to the end, then turn right. The freight bays are down there."

Cade walked along the passage. He reached the junction and followed the android's instructions. A few minutes later, directed by indicator panels, he found himself standing inside the freight-servicing bay. An assortment of craft was moored in the individual bays, some being worked on by crews of androids, others silent and deserted. The air was hot, and the crackle and blue flashes from welding arcs lit up the dark shadows. The rattle and hum of equipment rose and fell in irregular cadences.

Moving along the catwalk that ringed the service bays, Cade checked out the moored craft. In bay nine he found what he was looking for.

Lexus-6 was just under one thousand feet in length. It resembled a round-nosed cylinder in shape, with its flight deck at the tip and the huge engine pods housing the massive Mitsubishi ion-drive motors mounted on each side at the rear. Along the surface of the freighter's battered, streaked outer skin were numerous equipment pods, antennae and guidance dishes. One of the engine pods had been removed, exposing the port engine. The banks of ceramic cooling fins gleamed in the half light. Workdroids swarmed over the engine, fifty feet up from the service bay floor, operating from hydraulic gantries.

Cade saw that the main airlock was open, the freighter's interior lit only by access lights. He crossed from the catwalk to the bay extension, and from there to the airlock ramp. He slipped in through the airlock.

The freighter appeared deserted. Its main lights were off, leaving the companionways in shadow. Cade located the information board just inside the airlock. He checked the ship's layout, finding that the crew quarters were on deck three. If anyone was on board, that was the likely place to find them.

He made his way through the empty hulk of the freighter, finding and accessing the floor ramps until he was on deck three. Cade paused, trying to pick up a sound that might indicate the presence of any of the crew. The only thing he heard was the ponderous throb of the giant electric turbines working on reduced power and coming from deep in the bowels of the ship. They would be generating the electrical energy needed to keep the ship's ancillary equipment on standby.

Cade moved off again, stalking the companionways, his passage making no sound on the synthetic-rubber deck flooring. He checked out cabins and workstations, but apart from the soft pulse of light from equipment ticking over he saw and heard nothing.

He was becoming frustrated with his lack of success. Cade was trying not to allow his concern for Kate to affect him, but as time slipped away it was becoming increasingly difficult. He needed to know, one way or another, what had happened to her.

Then an android passed him ten feet away. It was moving with deliberate intent, carrying a tray holding a pot and mugs. Cade breathed in the aroma of coffee and saw the steam issuing from the pot. He watched the android moving away from him.

Hot coffee meant people on board, and people were a possible source of information.

Cade trailed the android as it progressed along the companionway. He stayed well behind, keeping to the shadows. It paused at a door that slid open at its approach and stepped inside the cabin.

Cade waited until the android returned, minus the tray. Once it had vanished along the companionway, he crossed to the door and waited for it to open. He slipped inside. He was in an empty crew room. Clothing was strewn around, and there were signs of recently eaten meals.

Through another door that stood slightly ajar, Cade heard voices. Snatches of conversation were interspersed with the odd burst of raucous laughter. He eased up to the door. The voices became clearer, and Cade picked out the odd phrase here and there.

He slipped the Magnum into his hand as a precaution as he eased through the door.

The cabin was a recreation lounge fitted out with comfortable reclining chairs and low tables. There was an audio center and a large-screen television-video player.

Three men were lounging in the recliners. The tray of coffee had been placed on the closest table. A number of empty beer cans lay on the table. No one had touched the coffee yet. The trio on the recliners was too absorbed in the picture on the television screen.

It was the image of a naked young female taking a shower. The picture quality was sharp and bright. Every detail had been recorded explicitly as the camera roved carefully and slowly up and down the lithe form of the woman.

Something caught Cade's attention as the woman turned, allowing the shower to rinse away the lather on her body. It was a familiarity in the form, in the subtle curves of the naked body. He told himself he was imagining things and that he was allowing his concern for Kate to distort what he was seeing.

But then the camera slid up over the curve of breasts he knew so well and focused in on the woman's face.

A hard, cold fist slammed Cade in the guts as he looked into the face of Kate Bannion.

For long moments he stood immobile, unaware that his hand was trying to crush the handle of the Magnum.

Through the white heat burning inside his skull, he heard the muttered lewd comments of the men in the cabin as they stared at the image on the screen. He heard their words and their laughter, and the world went crazy.

Cade wasn't aware of it but he was screaming like a maniac as he burst into the cabin, and the autopistol in his hand swung up in a target-seeking curve.

17

Cade saw one man roll out of his recliner, grabbing for the handgun on his hip. He was halfway across the cabin by then, his momentum carrying him forward in a wild rush. He met the man as he came up from a crouch, the gleaming autopistol trying to find a target. Cade fired first, putting a bullet through the left shoulder. The impact drove the man off his feet to the cabin floor, where he lay moaning, his dropped weapon forgotten in the wash of pain flooding his upper body.

A wild growl of anger filled Cade's ear. He twisted in time to meet the rush of the oncoming assailant. This one was big, clad in a stained T-shirt bearing the Lexus logo. His stocky body bulged against the taut cotton of the shirt, and Cade glimpsed heavy biceps above the muscular forearms. He slammed into Cade, driving him across the cabin. A pained grunt escaped Cade's lips as he was shoved bodily against the bulkhead, the back of his head rapping against the metal. The pain acted as a stimulant, and Cade batted aside the man's fist, then backhanded him with the autopistol. A howl followed the blow as the man pawed at the bleeding gash in his skull. When Cade kneed him hard in the groin, the howling increased as he bared his teeth in agony, staring up from watery eyes.

"I'm gonna rip your head right off...."

Cade jammed his elbow into his throat, feeling him gag, then whacked the Magnum's barrel down over the crew-cut skull, and the man went all the way to the floor this time.

The survivor came at Cade from the side. He had a knife in his hand and he slashed viciously, slicing the sleeve of Cade's jacket and opening a scorching gash in his arm. Cade twisted toward him, bringing up the Magnum, his finger steady on the trigger as he sought to ignore the image of Kate still on the TV screen, still naked, still washing, still rinsing herself off.

"Put the blade down, or you're finished," Cade barked. "Now!"

The man stared at death down the barrel of the massive autopistol and thought the better of it. He tossed the knife across the cabin, cursing Cade wildly.

Cade slammed the door shut, placing his back against the cold metal. He could still see Kate over the man's shoulder, and he felt the wildness rising again.

"Where is she?" he snarled. "And you'd better know."

"What? What are you talking about?"

"The girl in the video. She was on this ship. Where is she now?"

The man swung his head to look over his shoulder. "You mean her? Jesus, man, you should've said if that's all you wanted..."

Cade's foot lashed out with a blow, and the man crashed to the cabin floor, clutching his thigh and moaning. Cade knelt by him, then dragged his head up by the hair and thrust the .357 against his temple.

"Just be careful what you say next time," he said. "Now quit playing ignorant with me. You brought in a cargo of Darksiders?"

The man nodded, hardly able to speak.

"The girl in the video was on board, as well?"

There was another affirmative nod.

"Where is she now? And you'd better find your tongue this time."

"Somewhere in Six Domes."

"Where?"

"I don't know. That's where Pardee sent her after he questioned her. She told him she'd only been with the Darksiders for a day before we picked her up. No time to get too much on us."

"And?"

"Pardee...he roughed her up some...but she stuck to her story. In the end he figured she was telling the truth. So he had her dumped in Six Domes. In one of the brothels they run for the miners."

Cade's anger rose again. His finger began to squeeze the Magnum's trigger.

"No," the man screamed. "It's Pardee you want. Lexus security chief. He sent her. Said he didn't want her to die too fast. It was his idea of a joke. He's a sick son of a bitch."

"Where do I find Pardee?"

"He'll be in Six Domes. At the Ring."

"The Ring?"

"Club where they run fistfights. Out-of-work miners who need money. It's illegal, but everybody turns a blind eye."

Cade pushed him away. He stood up, his mind working frantically.

Kate *was* here, and she was in trouble.

He turned to leave, then paused. The Magnum swung in toward the TV set. Cade blew it apart, then did the same to the recorder below it.

"If you're thinking about calling Pardee to warn him—go ahead. Because I'd like him to know I'm coming to get him."

He left the ship, returning the same way he had entered the service bay. On his way back through the kitchen, the android he'd spoken to looked up.

"Did you give them a good report, too, sir?"

Cade shook his head. "No. They're a messy bunch. Garbage lying all over the floor."

The android looked suitably shocked.

Cade made his way to his car and swung it away from the port complex, picking up the road for Six Domes. He floored the pedal, sending the sleek vehicle full tilt along the smooth lane. There were no delays. When he reached Six Domes, he drove around until he spotted a group of miners heading for a noisy bar. He rolled the car to a halt and climbed out.

"Maybe you fellows can help me."

"Yeah?" one of the miners said. He eyed Cade suspiciously. "And maybe we can't."

Cade grinned. "Hey, don't give me a hard time, guys. I'm new around here. I need some directions."

"So where do you want to go?"

"I'm supposed to meet an old buddy of mine at some joint called the Ring. You know it?"

The hostile miner began to chuckle. "He wants to visit the Ring. You know what that place is?"

"Sure. Place where a guy can watch a good fight. Right?"

"Yeah. But it'll cost you plenty to find out where."

Cade was beginning to lose patience. He stifled his urge to lay one on the belligerent miner. Instead he pulled out a handful of bills and waved them under the guy's nose.

"It's important I get there."

The miner held out a big, scarred hand. "Gimme."

Cade peeled off a couple of hundred. He knew he was paying too generously but he didn't care, so long as it got him what he wanted.

"You that eager, maybe you'll hand over more," the miner said.

Cade's temper snapped. "You've more than enough for a few directions."

The miner grinned. He closed his fist over the money and started to turn away.

"More than enough to keep me in beer tonight. Now haul ass out of here, shithead."

Cade grabbed his shoulder and swung him around. He hit the miner once, crushing his nose with a hefty swing. The man went down howling amid a great gushing of blood, and the money fluttered to the ground. Cade scooped it up, then faced the miner's buddies. They were watching silently, offering no resistance.

"The offer stands," Cade said holding out the cash.

"Jenks always was a stupid mother," one of them said. He took the money and gave Cade his directions.

Back in the car, Cade checked the rear mirror and saw the miners hauling the groggy Jenks to his feet.

He drove through the deserted back streets, searching for the address he'd been given. It took him a good quarter of an hour.

Lexus City and Six Domes had changed a lot since his stretch with the Marine Corps. Then the place had been wilder, with little law and order. The asteroid was still under development and had the atmosphere of a frontier town. It was tamer now, but there was still the unruly element, with enough crime and violence to keep the security force busy—those who weren't on someone else's payroll. It was

the main reason why Cade and Janek had come in with fals
identities.

The Ring was located in a former dance club, and fron
the outside the place looked deserted. Cade parked the ca
and picked up the SPAS. He had a feeling he was going t
need some backup on this one. He approached from th
side. There was a guard on watch by the side door with a
squat SMG in his hands. He wasn't very good at his job
There was no concentration and even less alertness. Cade
managed to get within three feet before the guard realizes
he was being stalked. By then it was too late. The SPAS
looped around like a heavy black club. The man's head
whipped back, and his legs turned rubbery. He slumped t
the ground, rolling onto his face. Cade unloaded the SMG
and tossed it aside, then handcuffed the unconscious ma
and dragged him into the shadows on the far side of the site

The side door was unlocked, and Cade quickly slipped
inside. He was in a poorly lit corridor that ran deep into th
building. At the end there was a single door. Cade cracke
it open cautiously and peered into a bleak room that smelle
of sweat and disinfectant. There were a couple of benche
and a rickety table stained with dried blood. He crossed t
the door on the far side and opened it. There was anothe
corridor stretching before him. Now he could hear a dis
tant chant. Men shouting and yelling and whistling. Ther
was also the thump of many feet pounding on a floor.

He moved along the corridor. It angled sharply into a
wider passage with a slope leading into what appeared to b
pitch-darkness. The noise of the crowd had increased. Cade
followed the slope and emerged in a large room with a lov
ceiling where he sensed the presence of many people. The
only light in the place came from a couple of spotlights i

the center of the ceiling. They were focused on a single area in the middle of the room.

Cade stayed close to the wall, hidden by the shadows.

The baying crowd was gathered around a pair of men, stripped to the waist, who were beating each other senseless. Both men were already streaked with blood from numerous gashes and cuts to their battered faces, and livid bruises marked their sweaty torsos. The desperate pair threw heavy punches at each other as they stumbled and lurched around the blood-spattered circle formed by the crowd, oblivious to the howls and screams of the audience. The whole place reeked of fear and the barely restrained ill will of the crowd. It was so strong Cade could almost feel it.

He stood the grisly spectacle for as long as he could before he lifted the SPAS and triggered two shots into the ceiling. The thunderous roar of the combat shotgun cut through the scream of the crowd. As if it had been a single voice, the roar ceased, except for a few isolated words of protest.

"Plenty more where those came from," Cade yelled. "Justice Department. I want you people to listen to me. Give me what I want, and I'll leave you in peace. Screw around, and I'll give you more than a hard time."

The silence dragged on, broken only by the sound of the fistfighters who were still slugging it out.

"I don't have all night," Cade yelled.

"What do you want?"

"I want Pardee. Nobody else. Give him to me, and I'll leave."

"Give him the son of a bitch," somebody said. "I'm missing a good fight here."

A chorus of agreement rose from the audience.

"Dump the bastard."

"Hand him over. Company goon."

Somewhere in the crowd there was sudden commotion accompanied by shouting and cursing. Then a group of men emerged from the gloom, pushing a single figure before them, a lean, hard-faced man dressed in the uniform of Lexus Security. The name tag on his jacket identified him as Pardee.

"We don't mind if you lose him somewhere," a man called from the shadows.

"Put the sucker into orbit."

"You better take this."

An autopistol was thrust into Cade's hand.

Pardee stood glaring at Cade. His eyes were angry, threatening retribution.

The SPAS dropped level with Pardee's navel. "Let's go," Cade said.

Pardee moved ahead of him, away from the arena. He didn't say anything until the renewed roar of the crowd had faded.

"You want to tell me what this stupidity is about?"

"You're under arrest, Pardee."

Pardee laughed. "Come again?"

"Involvement in the illegal transportation of Darksiders from Earth."

Pardee spun around, ignoring the SPAS.

"Go screw yourself," he said. "I'm covered on that."

"You were until I busted Randolph Boon. Right now he's behind bars back in New York."

"How the—" Pardee's face tightened. "That bitch. So she did tip you off. And she had me believing she hadn't breathed a word to anyone. I should've hit her harder."

He was still speaking when Cade's boot slammed into his testicles. Pardee let out a high shriek. He doubled over, clutching at his groin, and Cade shoved his right knee into Pardee's face. The force of the blow straightened the security man up, slamming him into the wall. Blood streaked his lean face. Cade slugged him a couple more times, forgetting he was holding Pardee's gun in his left hand. He shoved the weapon under his belt, then reached down and hauled the man to his feet.

"Where is she, Pardee? Kate Bannion. Which brothel did you dump her in, you useless bastard?"

Pardee raised his battered head. Blood was dripping freely from his face. He tried to focus on Cade's angry eyes.

"I forget," he croaked, giving a lopsided grin.

"Then remember, pal, because I haven't even started yet."

Cade clamped a big hand over Pardee's collar and dragged him out of the building. He half carried the security man across to where he'd parked his car and dumped him on the ground. Pardee lay in a crumpled heap, breathing noisily through a broken nose. Cade left him for a minute before he dragged him to his feet and slammed him against the side of the car.

"Tough guy, huh?" Cade asked.

"Yeah."

"Specially when it comes to handling women. That it, Pardee? Your speciality?"

Pardee's lip began to curl. "I should have killed her," he yelled.

Cade hit him, letting go with all the frustration that was coming rapidly to a boil. The blow lifted Pardee off his feet and laid him out across the car's hood. Cade stuck the muzzle of the SPAS under Pardee's chin, grinding it into the flesh.

"You like to talk about killing other people, Pardee. How do you stand up to it yourself? You want to find out? Right now? All I need is one quick pull on the trigger, and you are gone. Hear me, Pardee? You really ready for it, you son of a bitch?"

The wildness in Cade's words convinced Pardee more than the feel of the SPAS burning into his flesh. The imminence of sudden death, never closer, unnerved him.

"Back off! For pity's sake, man. It's just not worth it, dyin' for a bitch like that. You want her that bad, you can have her. If you can get her back from Lange."

"Where?"

"I can show you."

Cade pulled Pardee to his feet and handcuffed him, then dumped him in the passenger seat of the car. Once he was behind the wheel, Cade placed the SPAS where Pardee could see it.

"Pull anything smart, and you'll be the first to get it. Guaranteed."

Following Pardee's direction, Cade drove west to the outermost section of Six Domes. This turned out to be the hardcore slum of the city where the dregs of Lexus existed in a gloomy twilight world. The dome had been one of the first to be built. It had basic facilities and had never been improved once the better-equipped domes had been constructed. As with any settlement created by man, there was always a need for the baser vices, and there were always those who would offer them. Here in Red Dome were the brothels, tolerated by the company because it accepted that it was probably safer if the miners, far from home and the majority living a single life, had the opportunity to legally relieve their sexual urges. The brothels, run with ruthless efficiency, were confined to Red Dome, as were the violent practices that always accompanied prostitution in its many and varied forms.

Entering the confines of the dome, Cade felt the oppressive aura of the place settle over him like a smothering blanket. He trailed along the twilight streets, passing bars and restaurants. The buildings were basic utilities, ugly and for the most part dirty. The same description seemed to fit most of the people Cade saw as he drove through the narrow streets.

"Turn down there," Pardee mumbled through swollen lips.

Cade pulled into the narrow street and followed it until it ended in a square. Facing him was a three-story building with malfunctioning neon sign at the front that said Lange's Place. Cade drew the car to a stop across from the place, noting the beefy bouncers loitering on the sidewalk outside the building.

Pardee seemed to find it amusing. He managed a throaty chuckle. "It'll be worth it just to see you get ripped apart."

"You'll have a long wait, Pardee," Cade advised.

He reloaded the SPAS, then did the same with the Magnum. He checked the Colt Stainless Steel .45 AutoSpecial he'd taken from Pardee.

"That should do it," he said under his breath.

"What the hell you going to do? Start a friggin' war?"

"Could be. I've handled these places back home, and one thing I know is they don't like giving up their girls. Only this time the girl happens to be somebody special. I want her back, and she'd better not be hurt, Pardee."

"Well, good luck, because you're goin' to need it. Man, this is going to be good. And I've got a ringside seat."

"Closer than you think," Cade said.

He climbed out and walked round to Pardee's side. He opened the door and hauled the security man out. Jamming the muzzle of the SPAS into the small of Pardee's back, Cade marched him across the square.

"Hey! What do you think you're doing? You can't drag me in there. They'll think I double-crossed them."

"Don't you worry. They'll know for sure when I tell them."

"Bastard," Pardee screamed. "You lousy—"

"Hey, what's going on?"

One of the bouncers blocked the way. He was broad and barrel chested. His unshaven face, pitted and scarred from too many contract periods down the mines, showed the hostility his voice expressed. His hand hovered close to the butt of a pistol shoved down the front of his pants.

"Get out of my way, or I'll make you," Cade said flatly.

The bouncer smirked. He began to close his fingers around the gun butt.

Cade rammed the SPAS into Pardee's spine, shoving him forward. The bouncer stepped aside to avoid the stumbling man, and Cade lashed out with the shotgun. It flashed twice. Once against his opponent's throat, then reversed as the stock crashed against his skull. The bouncer grunted and went down.

Out the corner of his eye Cade spotted another one dragging a compact SMG into line. He took a long step forward, then dived, hitting the surface of the street on his shoulder. His body twisted, bringing him around to face the bouncer, the SPAS already tracking in on its target. Cade fired once, the blast of the shot blanketing every other sound. The shot took the bouncer in the chest, spinning him off his feet and spiraling him to the ground. The stutter of an SMG blasted Cade's ears, and he felt the impact of the slugs against the street beneath him. He gathered his legs under him, thrusting himself up to his knees, picking up the gunman's position from the direction of the shots. Cade swept the SPAS around, catching a glimpse of the man as he tried to realign his weapon. Cade triggered the SPAS hard and fast, putting a wide blanket of shots in the area. The third blast caught the moving man, tearing him open along his spine and knocking him headfirst through one of the brothel's front windows. Cade gained his feet and moved toward the shattered window.

To one side Pardee had struggled to his feet and suddenly set off in pursuit of Cade.

The bouncer the Justice cop had put down lumbered sluggishly upright, shaking his bleeding head. He spotted Cade and dragged his handgun from the waistband of his pants. He let out a wild yell, leveled the gun and started to lay down a volley. He was firing on the move, his aim erratic.

Slugs chewed at the plastic window frame around Cade as he took a reckless dive through it.

Pardee was not so lucky. The security man was caught in the hail of slugs. He gave a startled cry as he felt the tearing impact of the bullets. They burned deep into his chest, cleaving his heart and lungs. Spitting bloody froth, Pardee stumbled over the window frame and crashed into the room.

Cade, back on his feet, crossed the room and kicked open the door. He was met by a hail of slugs that blasted the frame from the wall. He did a long belly flop, angling the muzzle of the SPAS toward the dark staircase where the shots had come from. The shotgun's powerful blast shredded the banister rails and peppered the hidden gunman. He sagged back against the stairs, then slid to the bottom in a loose heap.

On his feet again, Cade moved along the downstairs passage, kicking open doors and sweeping the interior of each room with the smoking SPAS. He disturbed the already panicking prostitutes and their clients, seeing more naked flesh in a couple of minutes than he usually saw in a month.

The only thing he didn't see was Kate Bannion.

He heard the thunder of feet from the floor above and angry voices demanding to know what was going on.

The bouncer from the street burst in through the front entrance, crashing along the passage. He opened up the moment he saw Cade, but his wild shots missed the mark. Cade dropped to a crouch and triggered the last two shells from the SPAS, slamming his opponent almost back out on the street.

Then he tossed the empty shotgun aside, and pulled Pardee's Colt and his own Magnum.

The footsteps above Cade ceased, a door opened to his left and a scared face peered out.

"I'm looking for a woman," Cade said.

"You came to the right place for that," the woman said. "But I think you got the idea wrong. You pay for 'em. Not force 'em at gunpoint."

"The one I'm looking for is new. She was brought in a few days back. Red hair. Name of Kate."

The woman smiled. "Well, she's a tough cookie, sure enough."

"Where is she?"

"Lange's got her up top in his own place. She gave everybody such a hard time he decided to break her in the hard way."

"How do I find it?"

"Just keep going up. Last flight of stairs, and it's the door facing you."

"Thanks."

"Hey. Watch out for the droids he keeps up there. They're nasty."

The woman withdrew behind the door, and he ducked low and hit the stairs on the run.

Shadows moved at the head of the stairs, light gleaming on raised weapons. Cade didn't wait. He opened up with his pair of autopistols, scything the stairs with a hail of shots. Men yelled. Bodies stumbled, crashed to the floor. Cade flattened as he reached the top, peering over the edge of the floor. A gun blasted close by, sending splinters flying. He ducked out of sight, heard the approaching footsteps and waited. A shadow fell over the stairs just ahead of him. Cade raised his Magnum, waited a couple more seconds, then pushed upright. He caught the man a fraction of a second off guard. The Magnum blasted twice, sending the .357 slugs slamming into the man's chest. He fell back with a trembling moan, twitching as he hit the hard floor.

The odd scream of panic coming from behind closed doors eventually faded away.

Cade went up the next flight slowly, remembering what the woman had told him. The stairs ended on a wide landing, with a single set of double doors ten feet in front of him.

Cade approached the doors slowly, his eyes searching, ears open for the slightest suggestion of sound behind them.

He was as close as four feet from the doors when he spotted the small security camera mounted in a corner of the ceiling.

"Shit!" he muttered, realizing he'd probably been monitored all the way up the stairs.

Before he could do anything else, the doors crashed open and a tall, chrometal droid came at him. It was fast for its size and bulk. Cade barely had time to duck as it cut the air with a powerful arm. The chrometal fingers snapped together in disappointment. Cade rolled, his move bringing him up behind the droid. On his back, Cade raised both feet and planted them against the robot's metal rear end. He straightened his legs. Caught off guard by the sudden move, the droid stumbled forward, missed its footing and toppled out of Cade's sight down the flight of stairs. Back on his feet, Cade moved to the head of the stairs in time to see the droid pick itself up and start to climb back up. He leveled the Magnum, aimed and fired in a single movement. The .357 slug cored through the droid's eye and cleaved its electronic brain apart. The droid faltered and lost its forward motion. Lurching drunkenly, it fell against the banister rail, smashed it and fell through to the floor below, where it lay twisting and jerking.

As Cade straightened up, he heard the heavy sound of the second droid. It blocked the doorway, its gleaming skull turning to pick Cade up with its keen eye. For the second time Cade recalled what Janek had done to stop the cybo back on the highway in New York.

He laid two shots through the droid's eyes. The slugs blew out through the back of the robot's head. It turned and walked into the wall just outside the doors before dropping with a heavy thump to the floor.

Cade entered the room. It was wide and expansive, with a curving picture window in the far wall. The floor space was cluttered with oversize armchairs, sofas and low occasional tables. Expensive electronic equipment lined one wall, and beneath the picture window was a huge circular bed covered with black sheets.

Cade's gaze was drawn by a stainless-steel cage that had been built in one corner of the room. The interior was bare, with no signs of any comfort being available for whoever happened to be in the cage.

A half-naked young woman occupied the cage, manacled in a half-sitting position. She could neither sit properly nor stand up. Held upright by the chains, the prisoner was forced to endure the uncomfortable and unnatural position for as long as the captor decided.

The face was hidden, but Cade recognized the supple outline and the red hair, though now it was tangled and matted, hanging loose over her face.

He didn't need to know any more. He had found Kate—and he had also found Lange.

The brothel owner was blond and tall, with a pale and narrow face that displayed a cruelness in the set of the mouth. His eyes were small, sharp and calculating. He was dressed all in black and wore knee-high boots that made him look taller and thinner than he was.

He uttered a wild howl of rage and lunged toward Cade with a thin-bladed knife. It sliced through Cade's shirt, the blade scraping the flesh of his chest.

"You've killed them! My most reliable guards! Murdered both of them!"

He hurled himself at Cade again, the glittering blade of the knife raised for another strike.

Cade threw up his arm to block Lange's descending knife hand. He struck hard, bruising the man's arm. Lange yelled with pain, then unexpectedly transferred the knife to his other hand and lashed out again.

Cade recoiled from the threat, his right hand shoving the muzzle of the Magnum against Lange's chest. He fired without hesitation, and the .357 slug tunneled through the brothel keeper's chest and erupted between his shoulders. Lange flew backward, crunching against the wall. He stared at Cade with a shocked expression and slid down the wall, falling forward on his face.

Cade ran to the cage and unbolted the door. He reached inside and started to release the manacles. He thought she was unconscious, but as he freed her from the last chain, she arched back from him, swinging her free arm in a wild punch that clipped his jaw.

"You won't have better luck this time!"

Her head came up, eyes locking with Cade's. She stared at him, seeing him but unable to accept what she was seeing.

Cade saw the ugly bruises on her face and body, the cuts and scratches, crusted with dried blood, and although the rage still made him tremble, he wanted to hold her close to make himself really believe he'd found her safe.

A soft, small sound rose in her throat. She reached out to touch him. "Cade?" she said hoarsely, and then her lovely face crumpled and she began to cry.

18

Accessing the mine complex proved easier for Janek than he'd imagined. Since there was nothing of great value in monetary terms to be stolen from the place, security was simple and straightforward. There were a couple of checkpoints on the approach road leading into the complex. Apart from those and a simple perimeter fence, the site was open. The titanium ore was unlikely to be stolen in any significant quantities, and even if it had been, there was little opportunity to get it away from Lexus-9.

Janek had memorized the mine layout from computer readouts and knew exactly how to approach the complex by the least noticeable route. He made his way to the extreme corner of the complex, where the fence ran close to the base of the dome under which it was housed. Here he was able to hurdle the fence with ease, landing well inside the grounds. He was in a section used to store worn-out machines employed in the underground operation. Janek worked his way through the abandoned equipment toward his destination, the air-recycling plant in the eastern sector of the complex.

Here the air from the generating plant was drawn through cleansing filters and pushed into the tunnels. This continuous process was maintained in order that the shifts of miners could be provided with clean, fresh air. It enabled them to work without the need for masks or oxygen tanks. The generating plant was housed in a large block, and according to the information Janek had absorbed, was operated by a team of androids. They were capable of working without

rest, monitoring the airflow and keeping the cleansing filters running at all times.

Janek had decided that he would use the air ducts to get
himself into the underground tunnels. His appraisal of the
layout had shown him which of the ducting systems he
needed to locate.

He wasted no time in completing his penetration of the
complex and reaching his access point. At the far side of the
generating plant were the massive ducting terminals. Clus-
ters of thick, corrugated aluminum pipes, six feet in diam-
eter, curved out from the side of the building. They ran
across the surface for some two hundred feet before angling under the surface of the asteroid. Janek's information had told him there were access hatches close to the place
where the pipes went underground. The cyborg's retentive
memory allowed him to recall the detailed information he
had absorbed and select the ducting pipe he wanted. Releasing the service hatch, Janek climbed inside, closing and
resealing the hatch behind him.

There were small emergency lights every fifty yards in case
urgent repair work needed to be carried out. The light they
provided was faint, but Janek was able to use his night-
vision facility to enhance the low illumination.

He crouched and moved along the pipe. When he reached
the section where the pipe angled sharply downward, Janek was able to use the corrugations to slow his descent. The
downward slope leveled out at three hundred yards, the pipe
stretching out ahead of him. He knew he had at least a
quarter of a mile to cover before he reached his destination.

Janek crawled along as the pipe leveled out. Unlike his
human partner, he had no need to rest. He kept up a steady
pace for the next half hour, then stopped. The main pipe
divided at this point. The right-hand junction continued its

journey to supply one of the regular tunnels. According to Janek's assessment, the left-hand pipe was a branch, angling sharply downward to the supposedly unworkable new seam. He took the left-hand pipe. It dropped for almost one-third of a mile before leveling off. From this point Janek only covered another five hundred yards before he was faced by the metal cabinet housing the filtration and booster unit that gave the air its final push into the tunnels. The main pipe continued on to feed other sections of the underground tunnel network.

Edging around the ten-foot-square cabinet, Janek reached the service hatch allowing access to the tunnel. He peered through the metal grille, scanning the dimly lit tunnel beyond. It appeared deserted. Opening the hatch, he eased his way through and dropped to the tunnel floor. He paused to close the service hatch before moving off along the tunnel.

It had been bored out of the solid strata by cutting machines, leaving an almost perfectly formed tunnel, ten feet high. Janek followed the tunnel for a few hundred yards before he noticed a distinct change in its formation.

The uniformity of the tunnel began to be marred by frequent erosion of the strata. Patches of broken rock and earth began to show. Bracing frames had been inserted to support sagging portions of the tunnel roof. The smooth floor became littered with debris that slowed Janek's progress. He moved ahead, his eyes adjusting to the gloom where the overhead lights had malfunctioned in sections. He became aware of faint sounds coming from deep within the strata itself. Restless groans and grating sounds as the strata moved and stressed. The sounds were beyond the range of the human ear, but his sensitive audio system was able to pick them up. He noticed the occasional trickle of dust sifting down from the roof of the tunnel—another indication of the area's instability.

Proof that Frakin's geology report had been correct. The mine company should have heeded his warnings and stayed out of the new seam.

The tunnel ahead began to curve. Janek rounded it and found himself confronted by a partial blockage where the wall of the tunnel had caved in. He studied the piled-up debris, locating the lowest point. Climbing the loose, shifting slope, he dragged away the uppermost rocks, expanding the gap so he could crawl through. Janek had no difficulty moving the heavy chunks of shattered rock. His only cause for concern was the damage the work did to the synthetic skin of his hands.

On the far side he noticed the tunnel widening and expanding. The air inlets feeding the tunnel became more frequent. Janek walked on. He began to pick up other sounds now, the scrape of metal on rock and mingled voices.

Minutes later Janek noticed that the tunnel ahead was becoming lighter. The sounds were getting louder, too. He spotted movement ahead. Pressing himself against the tunnel wall, Janek focused in on the vague shape. It sharpened into the form of a man. Clad in a dusty jumpsuit and wearing a hard hat, the man was armed.

Janek eased forward yard by yard, keeping close to the tunnel wall, watching the armed man as he wandered back and forth.

The tunnel began to widen. Janek found he was on the edge of a wide, circular cavern that had been carved out of the rock. It was at least thirty feet across, rising to a good fifteen feet high. Lights were embedded in the walls and ceiling, illuminating the area well.

Directly across from where Janek stood was a twenty-foot portable cabin. To the left a section of the cavern had been closed off by a chain-link fence. The fence reached to the roof of the cavern.

Janek saw a large number of people behind the fence. He estimated there were more than a hundred. He studied them carefully. Even allowing for the artificial atmosphere in the cavern, the captives had the same facial appearance. They all had the same pale, ghostly white flesh.

Janek had found his Darksiders.

A closer look showed a few young women in among the majority of men. They looked as haggard as the men.

Janek set the transmitter on a ledge some six feet up the tunnel side and activated the signal. Then he did the same with the unit in his pocket.

He moved back to the entrance to the cavern and checked the lone guard's movements. The guard had his back to Janek, and he was at the far side of the cavern where an open area looked out over a lower level.

Janek crossed the cavern on silent feet, coming up behind the unsuspecting guard. He struck the man above his ear, hard enough to stun him. From one of his pockets Janek produced a pair of plastic handcuffs. He secured the guard's hands behind his back, then dragged him into the shadows behind the cabin. Arming himself with the man's squat SMG, Janek checked out the cabin. It was deserted. The cabin was equipped with cooking facilities and a rest area. There was even a TV.

Outside the cabin Janek crossed to the secure compound. The Darksiders watched him with detached curiosity as he checked the locked gate in the fence. Closing his fingers over the lock, Janek wrenched it free and dragged open the gate.

The Darksiders remained where they were, still watching him silently.

"I don't expect to get trampled in the rush," Janek said. "But don't you want to get out?"

"Who are you?" a gaunt-faced man asked.

Janek pulled out his badge and held it up. "The name's Janek. I'm with the New York City Justice Department. Lexus has been busted over the hijacking of you people. The problem is they don't know that on Lexus-9, so the best thing we can do is get the hell out of here."

"What about the rest of us?" someone said. "Those already working."

"I haven't forgotten about them," Janek said. "How many guards are there?"

"Twenty. Maybe twenty-five."

"Don't forget the crew on the elevator."

"What kind of numbers are we talking about for those working?"

"Close to a hundred and fifty. Maybe less if there are any more cave-ins."

"Does that happen often?"

"Sometimes daily. Depends on how far into a seam we go."

A young man pushed his way to the front of the crowd. "How did you find out about us?"

"A tip-off. We followed it through until we had the whole story."

"Did you talk to our people back in New York?" the man asked.

"Yes. I went into the tunnels with my partner."

The young man's face gave away what he was about to ask. "I have a girl down there."

"Are you Harry?" Janek asked.

The man nodded vigorously. "Did you speak to...?"

"Lisa?" Janek said. "She helped us. And she told us about you. She's all right."

"Janek, get us out of here. Those bastards are killing us every day. All they want to do is get the titanium ore out before anyone discovers what they're up to. They make us work without safety gear. We have to dig the ore out with picks and shovels because they can't risk power tools. The tunnels are crumbling all around us.''

''How are they getting the stuff out without being discovered?''

''It's all a big cover-up. They have a makeshift loading dock at the far end of the main tunnel. It's on the far side of a range of hills so nothing can be seen from any of the domes. None of the regular miners know anything about us. They'd tear the place apart if they did.''

''Did they bring you in through this loading dock?'' Janek asked.

Harry nodded. ''We didn't know what was going on, and even when we did, what choice did we have? They told us from the start. Work or starve or get dumped out the airlock. They did that to a couple just to show they meant business. The mothers don't give a damn how many of us die.''

''Time we changed the odds,'' Janek said. ''There has to be a way out of here up to the domes.''

''There's an elevator,'' Harry said. ''The guards use it when they change shifts, but it's guarded and on a coded lock. They showed us in case anyone got ideas about breaking out.''

''Good,'' Janek said. ''Harry, can you use this?''

Harry took the SMG. ''One of the first things they teach you in the army.''

Janek turned to the assembled Darksiders.

''We're getting out of here. It isn't going to be easy. Those guards aren't going to walk away and let us. So there could be some trouble. Some of you will get hurt. But we have to release the rest of your people before we can leave.''

A muttering went through the Darksiders, but it was one of approval. ''So let's get to it.''

"I'd sooner die fighting than be buried under a rock-fall."

"Harry, I'll need you to guide me. The rest will have to stay back until we can gain a few weapons. Once we have the others free, we can make a break for the elevator."

Harry led the way across the cavern to the spot where the guard had been standing. It overlooked the main work area. In a gaping basin, twenty feet below where Janek stood, Darksiders worked ceaselessly under the watchful gaze of armed guards. A number of tunnels led off from the main area, and Darksiders could be seen entering and leaving these tunnels. They pushed ore trucks mounted on narrow rails. Loaded trucks were transferred onto a separate set of rails that vanished along a wider tunnel.

"That one goes to the loading dock," Harry explained. "The ore is dropped into a hopper that feeds into the cargo hold of a freighter. Very basic and simple, but it gets a lot of ore out. The shifts never stop. As soon as one finishes, a new shift starts."

"It's slave labor," Janek said. "And cheap for Lexus."

"Look," Harry said, pointing.

At the mouth of one tunnel a guard was beating a Darksider who had collapsed. The man, weak from the arduous work, offered no resistance. When he ceased moving, he was dragged to one side by the guard, who pushed another Darksider in to take up the workload.

"We lose so many that way," Harry said tonelessly. He stiffened suddenly. "Dammit, no more, Janek. No more."

"Wait," Janek said, but Harry had already moved, running for the sloping ramp that led to the lower level.

Janek followed, aware that the wheels had started rolling now. There was nothing he could do to stop it. He pulled his autopistol, slipping off the safety as he went after Harry.

Due to the dim light and the noise from the work in progress, Harry's descent wasn't noticed until he was almost at the bottom of the ramp.

Then one of the guards, turning to cross the floor, happened to glance in the direction of the ramp. He saw Harry, did a double take, but quickly recovered to raise a shout and open fire.

His shooting was noisy but inaccurate. The stream of slugs struck the rock wall over Harry's head. Harry threw himself off the ramp, landing behind a heap of debris.

Janek swung the big autopistol up, tracking the guard who was approaching Harry's hiding place. Stroking the trigger, Janek put hot lead through the guard's skull. The impact hurled the man to the ground, and the SMG bounced from dead fingers.

In seconds the whole area erupted. The Darksiders scattered as the guards opened up, firing on anything that moved. The cavern echoed loudly to the heavy bursts of autofire, the sounds amplified to the extreme.

Harry put his SMG to work, his first volley cutting down a pair of guards. The moment they hit the ground, Darksiders converged on them, using their digging tools as they made sure they wouldn't give any more trouble.

As Janek reached the end of the ramp, he was faced by a guard who had just burst out from one of the tunnels. Janek responded first, triggering his autopistol. The powerful weapon drove a pair of bullets into the guard's chest. He staggered, slamming into the wall at his back. Before he hit the ground, a Darksider was on him, using his shovel as a club to batter the man's skull.

Stone chips exploded from the rock face inches from Janek. He lunged forward, bodily slamming into a pair of Darksiders who were in range. One fell clear, but the second man gave a stunned cry as burning bullets chewed into the flesh of his upper chest. The man tumbled back, clawing at the fatal wounds, his hands turning red. Crouching over the Darksider he had pushed clear, Janek swung his autopistol across his body, triggering a fast trio of shots at the guard who had fired the deadly volley. The impact picked the guard up and tossed him aside.

Behind Janek the Darksiders he had freed started down the ramp, oblivious to the danger from the guards' weapons.

Underfoot, Janek felt the floor tremble, then he felt something drop against his shoulder. Glancing up, he saw dust trailing down from the cavern roof. Focusing his eyes on the roof, he spotted fine cracks spreading across the rock. The floor rippled beneath his feet.

It was the heavy bursts of fire from the guards. The amplified vibrations were disturbing the fragile hold of the strata.

Janek made his way across to where Harry crouched.

"Now it's our turn," Harry said.

"Harry, we have to get out fast. The cavern is starting to break up. The gunfire is disturbing the faulty strata. This place could come down on us any minute. We have to pass the word and get everyone out."

Harry stared at him with wide eyes. "There's no damn way we can get them all in the elevator. It only takes a few at a time."

"It's all right," Janek said. "I have a better idea for getting us out."

"What?"

"The ore freighter. There's enough room in the thing to fly all your people. We can take it up to Platform-12. There's a Marine Corps unit based there. A squad is on its way down now to help, but I don't think we can wait. We have to get out now."

The Darksiders from the ramp were spreading across the cavern with weapons taken from the dead guards. Harry broke cover, moving from group to group, passing the word. Darksiders went into the working tunnels to warn those inside.

Janek hurriedly headed for the main tunnel, conscious of the increase in the rockfall from overhead. Dust was sifting in a constant stream now, accompanied by debris.

A yelling guard slammed into him, lashing out with his empty weapon. The barrel of the SMG caught Janek across the side of the face. It tore his synthetic skin and exposed the dull gleam of titanium beneath. The guard stared at the metal, and in that moment of hesitation Janek put a slug into him, blowing the man off his feet.

Harry reached the mouth of the tunnel almost at the same time as Janek. He was waving his people into the tunnel, yelling at them to hurry. Somewhere in one of the working tunnels a deep rumble sounded, followed by the crash of falling rock. Seconds later a thick cloud of dust erupted from the mouth of the tunnel, billowing out across the cavern. Men scattered in panic, some being swallowed in the dust. Overhead there was a loud crackle of splintering rock. Large chunks began to fall, some of them splitting as they hit the cavern floor.

Janek heard men screaming in fear and pain.

He waited for the dust to clear and searched the littered cavern floor. A number of bodies lay sprawled beneath chunks of rock. Others were stumbling blindly over the debris, still trying to reach the safety of the tunnel.

"There," Harry yelled above the din of falling rock and sporadic gunfire.

Janek saw the Darksider pinned by his legs. Without a second's hesitation he headed for the trapped man, ignoring the falling rock that struck him. Reaching the man, Janek bent over him, jamming his gun back in its holster.

"Save yourself," the injured man said. "No one can shift that damn rock."

"You got cash to make a bet on that?"

He dug his hands under the edge of the slab of rock and lifted. Beneath the flexi-coat of titanium, Janek's powerful servo-muscles took the strain. The slab of rock lifted with ease, and the Darksider was able to drag himself clear. One leg was badly crushed and bloody.

"Come on," Janek said, "let's get the hell out of here."

He picked the man up and carried him back to where Harry stood watching.

Two Darksiders took the injured man and headed along the tunnel, following the mass of Darksiders already jamming the way.

Janek pulled his gun, turning on his heel as a stream of bullets scored the tunnel wall close by. He slapped Harry's shoulder, knocking the man to the floor. Armed guards were running in the direction of the tunnel, as though they intended reaching the protection of the freighter themselves.

Janek opened fire. His spaced shots took out two of the hostile guards, dumping them on the hard floor of the cavern. The surviving pair concentrated their fire on Janek's position. Bullets chipped the rock around him, and he felt a couple slap against his torso, pushing him off balance for a second. Lifting his autopistol, Janek returned fire. He caught one guard. The other got to his feet and turned to run, but Harry emptied his magazine into him before he'd taken two steps.

They were free again to head along the tunnel. Behind them the sound of falling rock increased.

Harry glanced at the tall, blond-haired figure, and a smile touched his lips.

"You're not your usual cop," he said.

The rattle of gunfire from the front of the massed crowd caught Janek's attention. He began to push his way through the packed crowd.

"They won't let us near!" a man yelled.

"The bastards want us dead."

"Let's rush 'em."

Janek was able to see over the heads of the Darksiders and spotted the five armed guards blocking the end of the tunnel. Beyond them was the bulk of the freighter, resting against the loading platform of the dock. At the extreme end of the dock was the airlock that had been built into the solid rock-face. As he pushed his way to the front, he felt the tunnel floor shift. Janek saw an autoweapon in the hands of a weary, unshaven Darksider. The man wasn't even aware he still had the weapon. Easing the weapon free, Janek checked the magazine. The indicator told him it was full. He snapped back the cocking lever and stepped free from the crowd.

"Let them through," he ordered. "I'm a marshal from the Justice Department. Don't waste any more lives. This operation is all finished."

"Says who?" one guard sneered.

"I do," Janek told him.

The guard peered at Janek, seeing the dull metal gleaming through his torn skin.

"Jesus, it's a fuckin' robot. Giving us orders."

He began to laugh as he moved forward, raising his SMG.

Janek sighed wearily. They never learn, he thought.

The autoweapon in his hands swept up with terrible precision. Janek's finger touched the trigger, and the SMG began to crackle with fire.

The lead guard was the first to die, his body shredded by the unerringly accurate fire. Before his bleeding, torn body hit the ground, Janek had swiveled the SMG, laying down a withering blast of fire that swallowed the other guards in its deadly maw even as they loosed a few shots that sent injured Darksiders tumbling to the ground. They were hurled back across the dock, bodies trailing blood and shredded flesh. The SMG snapped on an empty breech, smoke curling from the muzzle. Janek tossed the weapon aside, shaking his head at the guards' stupidity.

He stood and watched as over three hundred Darksiders swarmed through the freighter's open airlock and into the cargo holds.

Harry nudged him and leaned closer. "Hey, Janek, let's get out of this damn place before we get buried along with the rest of the garbage." As they went on board, Harry suddenly asked, "Can you fly this damn thing?"

Janek grinned. "Can a hen lay eggs? Come on up to the flight deck and watch a goddamn tin man fly this bird."

19

"I can't believe it! After everything I went through!"

Kate threw down the copy of the newspaper. It slid across Cade's desk, and he had to snatch up his mug of coffee before it landed in his lap.

"They killed my story, T.J. All I got was a half column on the sixth page." She slumped in a chair across from him, her eyes blazing with anger.

Milt Schuberg cleared his throat self-consciously. He was standing at the window, pretending to watch the clouds drifting by.

"I guess you guys are feeling pretty pissed off about this," he said.

"Nobody's blaming you, Milt," Cade told him.

"Hell, I lost, too," Schuberg said. "When Boon walked, I wanted to..." He shrugged. "What could I do? The guy has clout that goes all the way back to Washington Central. The big boys were all gunning for us. Too many behind-the-scenes manipulators."

"Most of them in Boon's pocket," Janek said.

"Let's face it," Schuberg added. "There are a lot of people making fortunes out of this titanium bonanza, including the armaments business. They couldn't afford to stop bringing the stuff in."

"Boon might have walked free, but at least we put a stop to him exploiting the Darksiders," Janek said. "And security on Lexus-9 has been tightened up."

Bronson and his Marines had swept through the Lexus mine complex on their arrival, taking out the resistance offered by the guards involved in the Darksider affair. In the aftermath, once the story had come out, the miners had staged a walkout until new management was installed and the dangerous seam closed off. Bronson's men had discovered a mass grave where dead Darksiders had been buried. The body count reached over two hundred. To Bronson's disgust, the facts had eventually been suppressed and a cover story put out.

By the time Cade, Janek and Kate arrived back in New York, the shouting had all but died down. The returned Darksiders had been sent back to their tunnels, despite a strong desire to have their grievances aired.

Randolph Boon, out on bail, was on his estate in the Bahamas. Clever manipulation of the media by his lawyers had diverted much of the publicity away from him. Lesser employees in the Lexus conglomerate were taking the fall for Boon's nefarious scheme. As he was unable to answer back, the dead UCS captain, Connor, had been cited as having a great deal of responsibility for the crimes. UCS, always a thorn in the side of the NYPD because of its backing by local politics, had come under close scrutiny, and much of its power had been taken away.

The overall results were less than satisfactory for those most involved.

Schuberg had his prime suspect freed on bail and had to live with the knowledge that Boon was unlikely to stand trial.

Kate Bannion, having survived her ordeal on Lexus-9, was finding that the power of the press was not always beyond the heavy hand of governmental repression.

The Darksiders, who had suffered more than most, recognized betrayal and retreated to their subterranean world. They saw clearly that justice was not going to be served in their cause.

Cade seemed to accept the lesser victory better than anyone. He was angry, even bitter. The Justice Department, though fighting the court decision on Boon, seemed to be losing. Orders had come from Washington Central for Cade to step back from the affair and move on. He took that as a polite way of being warned off. He didn't like it, but he appeared to have accepted it.

His partner didn't believe it for a second. Janek said nothing, but looked and listened a lot. He knew better than to accept Cade's meek surrender. There was something going on in Cade's head that was removed from his everyday activities, and Janek was curious to know what it was.

"Milt, you going my way?" Kate asked suddenly.

Schuberg grinned. "Anytime, honey," he said.

"T.J.?" Kate said. "I'll see you later?"

He glanced at her. "I'm not sure." He patted a file on his desk. "Something I have to look into first."

"Looks like it's back to business," Schuberg said.

"Give me a call," Kate said. She leaned over and kissed him on the cheek. "I haven't had time to thank you properly for pulling me out of Lexus-9," she added in a low whisper.

Cade grinned up at her. "You will."

She spread her hands. "Sorry about blowing off steam, guys," she apologized. "It was only a story."

Janek didn't say anything until the door had closed behind Kate and Schuberg. He came around to sit across from Cade, his eyes boring into his partner's.

"Give, T.J. I want to know what you're up to."

Cade remained impassive. "Me? What could I be up to, partner?"

Janek waved a finger at him. "That's what I want to find out."

"I'VE A BAD FEELING about this, T.J."

"Get us down," Cade said. "These coordinates."

"I can read a map, Thomas," Janek said in a hurt tone.

The cyborg eased back on the stick of the sleek, matt black helicopter. The machine had twin turbo-powered motors that could drive it along at over 250 mph. Now that they were within striking distance of their target, Janek had engaged the silent-running mode, reducing the chopper's engine noise to a subdued whisper.

Below them the calm waters of the Florida Strait gleamed dully under a pale moon. Ahead lay Grand Bahama Island.

"Down, buddy," Cade said. "Just in case somebody left the radar on."

Janek angled the chopper until it was skimming the waves. He flew parallel with the sandy coastline until the marker on the chopper's computer screen flashed to show they were within a half mile of their target.

Minutes later Janek eased the helicopter to a gentle landing on the white beach. He cut the engines. As he and Cade climbed out, they could hear the soft hiss of the ocean rolling in against the shore.

Both of them were clad in black jumpsuits. Their faces were blacked, and they wore dark gloves. Janek had a black wool cap pulled over his pale hair.

"The villa is over there," Cade said. "The other side of those trees."

"Are you sure about all this?" Janek asked.

"Would I drag you into trouble?" Cade asked. "Trust me, partner."

"Every time I do, I regret it," Janek grumbled.

They slipped through the stand of swaying palms. Tall grass curved out of the sand, slapping at their legs as they passed by. Beyond the trees they could make out the rooftop of the spacious villa. It stood in its own grounds, surrounded by a steel-mesh fence.

Crouching at the fence, Cade tapped Janek on the shoulder. "All yours," he said.

"I'm sure this is highly illegal," Janek mumbled as he checked the fence for sensors and electro-beams.

"Leave the worrying to me," Cade said.

"Sensors," Janek confirmed. "And before you ask, Thomas, yes, I can override them."

He bent to the task, tapping in to the sensor's frequency, then splicing in an override chip. Once he had that completed, Janek used a small pair of cutters to open a gap for them to slip through. He eased the section back into place in case anyone wandered by.

Cade led the way across the wide, smooth lawn, dotted with exotic plants and tall palms. The villa ahead was ablaze with light, throwing long shafts out across the grass.

"Did your informant tell you how many armed guards we might run into?" Janek asked.

"Four patrolling the grounds," Cade answered. "Another three inside the house."

"For an innocent man, our friend Boon appears to be worried."

"That's the point, Janek. The son of a bitch isn't innocent. He's guilty as hell."

"Then why is he here and not in jail?"

"Because we live in an unfair world. Money and influence still talk. If you've enough of both, you get away with murder. In Boon's case, mass murder."

"I thought that was why the Justice marshal units were formed. To make sure people like Boon don't get off."

Cade grinned in the darkness. "Right. And that's what we're doing. Our job."

He placed a hand against Janek's chest, cautioning him.

An armed figure had strolled out of the shadows near the villa. The guard angled across the grass, not seeing the intruders but coming directly for Cade and Janek.

Reaching under his left arm, Cade drew the dull black gun holstered there. He took quick aim and fired. The gun only made a soft hiss. It fired a sleeper dart. The guard grunted as the needle point pierced his neck. He took two more steps before the powerful drug took effect. He sprawled face down on the grass, and Janek dragged him out of sight beneath a sprawling mass of vegetation. They repeated the operation twice more within the next few minutes.

Cade and Janek sprinted toward the side of the villa. Flattened against the outer wall, they checked the area. Nothing moved.

"Let's go," Cade said.

They eased along the wall until they reached a side door. It opened at Cade's touch, and they slipped through. They found themselves in the spacious garden laid out at the rear of the villa. It was a mass of flowers and lush vegetation, and closer to the house was a huge swimming pool. A number of athletic, sun-bronzed girls were cavorting naked in the water.

"Don't look," Cade warned his partner. "They'll corrupt you."

"You're looking," Janek whispered.

"Yeah, well, it's too late for me."

They worked their way to the rear of the villa by way of the wall and the concealing vegetation.

A flight of stone stairs led up the side of the villa to a balcony fronting an upstairs room.

"Boon's study," Cade said.

They climbed the stairs, keeping out of sight below the stone wall that edged the steps.

Sliding glass doors closed the comfortable room off from the balcony. Peering round the edge, Cade spotted Randolph Boon seated behind a massive desk, working on some papers. He was not alone. An armed guard was with him.

"Boon's in there," he told Janek. "Behind the desk to the left. There's a guy with an SMG. He's on the far side of the room. I want to do this fast, Janek. No chance for either of them to raise any alarm."

"I'll deal with the guard," Janek said, drawing his own gun.

He leaned around the edge of the glass door, scanning the interior of the room and pinpointing his target. Janek closed his hand over the edge of the door and slid it open. The door ran on smooth rails, opening without a sound, and by the time the guard realized there was an intruder it was too late.

Janek stood in the doorway, his right arm tracking the guard with his gun. He touched the trigger, feeling the weapon push back as it fired. The shot struck the guard under the chin, and the slender dart expended its drug swiftly into the bloodstream.

Randolph Boon's first awareness of something being wrong came when he saw the guard stagger and fall. Boon pushed his chair away from his desk, half rising. He turned and saw the two black-clad figures framed in the open doorway.

Cade stepped into the room, raising his weapon.

"For God's sake," Boon said. "You can't..."

Cade fired. The dart pierced Boon's expensive silk shirt and dug into his flesh. The tycoon felt the rush of the drug through his body. The room began to dissolve before his eyes. He tried to remain on his feet, clutching at the edge of his desk. The desk slipped away from his fingers, and his body lost contact with reality. Boon felt he was drifting, floating. The room disappeared, and he was in limbo....

BOON OPENED HIS EYES, blinking with the effort. He felt disoriented. Strange sounds and smells invaded his senses. He realized he was sitting on cold, hard earth. He raised his hands to rub his aching, blurred eyes, and felt dirt on the palms and on his fingers.

He saw his surroundings swim into focus.

He was in some kind of crude room, or was it a cave? There was a blanket covering the entrance. The light was dim. Boon sniffed. The smell was terrible. It was like the lingering smell of long-ago-decayed food and human waste.

He touched his head. Where in hell was he? He was deeply puzzled and wondered if he were dreaming.

Boon become aware that he wasn't alone.

He turned slowly, hesitantly.

Pale, white faces stared at him. Eyes that gleamed with undisguised hatred.

"Who are you?" Boon demanded. His voice rasped in his dry throat. "And where am I?"

"You are in your future," someone said. "But I wouldn't bank on it being a comfortable one."

"I don't know what you're talking about," Boon said. He tried to stand up, but his legs wouldn't support him. "Do you people know who I am? If this is some kind of extortion, you'll regret it. I promise you that."

"No, Boon, you won't get out of this one with money or influence. We don't acknowledge those things. We have our own laws. And here the guilty are punished."

"Guilty? Of what, damn you."

"Of murder," a voice close by whispered. "Mass murder."

A cold hand clamped over Boon's heart. "Where am I?" he asked again, only this time the arrogance had gone from his voice.

"You are with us," the whispered voice said. "We are the Darksiders, Randolph Boon, and you have been delivered into our hands for true justice to be served."

Boon stared about him at the pale faces and the dark accusing eyes, and he knew he was lost. His money. His powerful friends. The fear he instilled in others. None of it meant a thing down here. Not with these people and the need they had to see simple justice done, without the benefit of the long and uncertain legal system.

"Stand up, Boon, and come with us. We have a long way to go yet. To the lowest levels, where you will be tried and convicted."

"If you're going to kill me, why not get it over with?" Boon protested.

"Oh, no," the whisper said. "We won't kill you, Boon. You will be allowed to live out your life until a natural death claims you. But you will live it out in the darkest, deepest tunnels known to us, where no daylight ever penetrates. That's where you will serve your sentence, Boon, and believe it now. You'll never see your world ever again."

Rough hands pulled Boon to his feet. He was ushered through the blanket and along a narrow, damp tunnel on the first steps of his long journey to the depths of the Darksiders' world.

He didn't notice the two figures who watched him go, or hear one of them speak.

"And that, partner, is justice," Cade said.

Janek thought about it and realized it was.

Real justice.

These heroes can't be beat!

Celebrate the American hero with this collection of never-before-published installments of America's finest action teams—ABLE TEAM, PHOENIX FORCE and VIETNAM: GROUND ZERO—only in Gold Eagle's

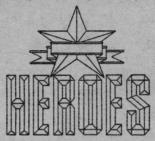

Available for the first time in print, eight new hard-hitting and complete episodes of America's favorite heroes are contained in three action-packed volumes:

In **HEROES: Book I**   July $5.99   592 pages

ABLE TEAM: Razorback by Dick Stivers
PHOENIX FORCE: Survival Run by Gar Wilson
VIETNAM: GROUND ZERO: Zebra Cube by Robert Baxter

In **HEROES: Book II**   August $5.99   592 pages

PHOENIX FORCE: Hell Quest by Gar Wilson
ABLE TEAM: Death Lash by Dick Stivers
PHOENIX FORCE: Dirty Mission by Gar Wilson

In **HEROES: Book III**   September $4.99   448 pages

ABLE TEAM: Secret Justice by Dick Stivers
PHOENIX FORCE: Terror in Warsaw by Gar Wilson

Celebrate the finest hour of the American hero with your copy of the Gold Eagle HEROES collection.

Available in retail stores in the coming months.   HEROES

World War III is only moments away in . . .

DON PENDLETON'S
THE EXECUTIONER®
FEATURING MACK BOLAN®

STORM BURST

In the final instalment of the STORM TRILOGY, Mack Bolan faces an Arab-Soviet conspiracy terrorizing the free world. The Executioner, along with Able Team and Phoenix Force, race to prevent a nuclear showdown that threatens to explode—literally—across the globe.

GOLD EAGLE

S8-27

A storm is brewing in the Middle East and
Mack Bolan is there in . . .

THE STORM TRILOGY

Along with PHOENIX FORCE and ABLE TEAM, THE
EXECUTIONER is waging war against terrorism at home
and abroad.

Be sure to catch all the action of this hard-hitting trilogy
starting in April and continuing through to June.

Available at your favorite retail outlet, or order your copy now:

Book I:	STORM WARNING (THE EXECUTIONER #160)	$3.50	☐
Book II:	EYE OF THE STORM (THE EXECUTIONER #161)	$3.50	☐
Book III:	STORM BURST (352-page MACK BOLAN)	$4.99	☐

	Total Amount	$ _____
	Plus 75¢ Postage ($1.00 in Canada)	_____
	Canadian residents add applicable federal and provincial taxes.	
	Total Payable	$ _____

Please send a check or money order payable to Gold Eagle Books to:

In the U.S.
3010 Walden Avenue
P.O. Box 1325
Buffalo, NY 14269-1325

In Canada
P.O. Box 609
Fort Erie, Ontario
L2A 5X3

Please Print:
Name: _____
Address: _____
City: _____
State/Province: _____
Zip/Postal Code: _____

GOLD
EAGLE

ST92-1